MARCH TO THE MONTERIA

MARCH TO THE MONTERIA

B. TRAVEN

a&b

This edition published in Great Britain in 1996 by
Allison & Busby Ltd
179 King's Cross Road
London WC1X 9BZ

First published by Allison & Busby in 1982

A catalogue record for this book is available from the
British Library

ISBN 0 74900 214 X

Printed and bound in Great Britain by
WBC Book Manufacturers Ltd
Bridgend, Mid Glamorgan

March to the Monteriá

THE AUTHOR

No one knows who B. Traven really was. He was probably German, but B. Traven was almost certainly not his true name. It was thought he may have been a man called Hal Croves who died in 1969, but he was also linked to the name Torsvan, which was believed to be a Traven Alias. A BBC programme over a decade ago was no more successful in getting at the truth of his identity. But one fact we do know: he did live in South America. Whoever he was, there is no disputing that he is widely remembered for his *Treasure of the Sierra Nevada* and his six *Jungle Novels*, of which *March to the Monteriá* is the third, about the conditions that led to the peasant uprising in Mexico in 1910.

1

 The Chamula Indian, Celso Flores, of the Tsotsil nation, had a girl in Ishtacolcot, his native village. He could have snatched her up and eloped with her, but he did not do that because of his respect for the girl's father. And the father, following the ancient custom of his tribe, could not simply give away his daughter. Before the eyes of his tribesmen the marriage would not have been considered legal, even if it had been legalized by a civil judge whose authority nobody acknowledged anyhow.

The girl was pretty, strong and healthy. Her father was convinced she would easily bear her man fifteen children, perhaps more. So it was only natural that her father asked a fair price for giving his daughter away.

Celso offered to work three years for the father to get the girl. But the old man wanted something more tangible, something more substantial. He insisted on six healthy, grown sheep, fifteen yards of white cotton goods, two quintales of worm-free corn, twelve muñecas of raw tobacco and two gallons of aguardiente.

That much Celso could never earn in Ishtacolcot where hired labor was unknown. So nothing else remained for him to do but to get himself a contract to work at a coffee plantation somewhere in the region of Soconusco, one hundred and fifty miles away from home, as the bird flies.

After two years of sweating, groaning and saving, he managed to collect a fair amount of honest, hard silver pesos. It looked good and was pure silver but it certainly had come hard.

Work at a café finca is the next worse thing to work in a montería. You work from sunrise to sunset, with no holidays and rarely a free Sunday. At harvest you are paid by the basket and before you have picked a hundred baskets, brother, you've had to move your buttocks about. When the overseer, the so-called capataz or cabo, decides to see too many green beans in your basket, that basket is not chalked up. He just throws the whole load on the pile without crediting you and so you have picked the whole basket for free. The owner or the manager of the plantation does not throw away those beans, of course. And why should he? He has to look after his business. Little Indian children under five pick out the green beans.

Anyway, two years of Celso's life had passed and, in possession of the money he needed to get married, he found himself on his way home.

Now, in Celso's native land, the shortest is the most difficult route by which to reach home.

He went by way of Niquivil and Salvador and so had to pass through several villages. In each village the alcalde, or mayor, charged him ten centavos for the right to pass through. And when he had to cross a bridge, even if it was decrepit and practically out of use, some authority, or whoever claimed to be an authority, took twenty centavos from him for bridge toll. Of course, wherever it was possible he looked for a path by which he could avoid a village.

All along the road he was offered contraband liquor. This bootleg stuff was more expensive than the kind sold legitimately, and of the worst possible quality. Everywhere someone tried to get the boy drunk, so he could be thrown in jail. When a drunk got up in the morning to continue on his way, he had no money left, not a single centavo, and if he complained that his money had been taken away from him by the chief of police, he was sentenced to three months of forced labor in the village or on the road for contempt of authority.

Celso, however, had learned enough at the plantation from the experiences of his fellow workers. He did not take a drop, even when it was offered out of pure friendship.

Whatever he needed on his way was sold to him at three or four times the regular price. Wasn't he a cafetal worker returning home, a very rich youngster with his pockets full of good money?

But here, too, he was astute and obstinate. He walked along in old rags and did not tell a soul that he was returning from the cafetales. When some storekeeper or local authority demanded to know where he came from, he said that he had taken four mules to Huixtla for his patrón in Jovel.

Jovel was the last town through which he had to pass to reach his native village and it was only about twelve miles from it.

In Jovel he already felt at home. At least twice a month he had visited Jovel with his father and mother to sell or trade corn, wool, fruit, firewood, raw skins or chile. Now he bought five centavos worth of bananas from an Indian woman who had spread her wares on a mat in the portico of the municipal building. He crossed the street and squatted on his haunches on the bare ground of the square, ignoring the dozens of benches around the plaza.

These benches were reserved exclusively for ladinos, the civilized population of the town. Of course, this civilization did not extend, in all cases, to the degree where everybody felt obliged to wash and shave every morning. Such superfluous matters could well wait until Sunday without loss of the right to be considered a ladino.

Celso, a stray Indian, would have been chased away by the police had he dared to sit down on one of the empty benches. But the police did not even chase away stray dogs from the plain, stone-paved ground of the plaza. Consequently Indians in need of a rest were allowed to squat on the curb.

On one of the benches sat two ladinos. Caballeros, they were called. They sat smoking their cigarettes and criticizing the state government.

Said one of the caballeros: "This town is full of certain people who don't even deserve to have a shirt to cover their dirty behinds and who put on airs as if they owned the whole damned town. And then there are others like that Chamula youngster over there, on his haunches, stuffing himself with bananas. He looks as if you have to give him a centavo to keep him alive. And yet that dirty bastard has nearly eighty silver pesos wrapped up in his sash."

"How come you are so well informed?" asked the other caballero.

"He's from my finca where he worked for two years in my cafetales. Celso is his name. He's the son of Francisco Flores in Ishtacolcot."

"Really? You don't say."

"Of course. But what do I care about that worm. What I actually would like to know is how many thousands and thousands of shining pesos that good-for-nothing governor has pocketed by now for the road to Arriaga, and how many thousands and thousands of pesos will he continue to pile up for himself before it will be possible to really travel safe and sound on that road. But the matter is . . ."

The other caballero was not interested in the thousands of pesos collected by the governor for a road that would never be built, or if it would be built, would be constructed so badly that it would have to be completely rebuilt after every rainy season, thus giving him an opportunity to collect thousands of pesos again, levied as special taxes, so-called cooperatives. The caballero, in the shoes of the governor, would do exactly the same thing. But since, for the moment, he was not the governor, he had to look for some other method to collect his pesos. He no longer listened while the government was being cursed, but instead shouted across the square at Celso: "Hey, you, Chamula, come over here."

Celso turned around, and when he saw it was a ladino who shouted at him, he jumped up and hurried toward the caballero. The bananas, which he had just started to eat, were left abandoned on the curb.

He stood before the caballero, politely took off his palm hat, and said: "A sus órdenes, patroncito, at your service."

"You know me, don't you?" said the caballero.

"Sí, patroncito, of course I know you. You are Don Sixto."

"Right. And I've sold your father two young oxen. Only part he has paid. And your father has under a sacred oath promised me, with a guarantor, Cornelio Sánchez, whom you also know, that he would pay me the balance on the same day you returned from the coffee finca with your money. That balance is exactly seventy-six pesos and fifty centavos. Hand over the money so that your father won't have to make the long trip into town. Is that matter of the debt correct, Don Emiliano?" Don Sixto asked his friend.

"The debt is correct and duly guaranteed," replied Don Emiliano.

For a moment it occurred to Celso that Don Emiliano could not very well know whether the matter of the debt was correct, because he had seen Don Emiliano still at home, on his coffee finca, only a few days ago. But at the same time he also knew that against the word of a caballero the word of an Indian was no good. If the caballero said the earth turns around the sun, the Indian had to accept it as the truth, even though it was evident to his eyes that the sun turned around the earth. Thus it was in all matters which a caballero affirmed. And in this particular case there were two caballeros affirming something which he could not know because he had not been home for two whole years.

However, he was not given any chance to think or to reflect upon what he had just heard.

Don Sixto proceeded rapidly. "Come across with the money, muchacho," he said in a cold and pitiless voice. "If you refuse to pay, I'll call the police, and you'll have time in jail to think over what a duly guaranteed debt means."

From the experience of many of his kinfolk Celso knew very well how expensive jail could be for an Indian. They would take the money away from him, because he could not hide it. And on top of that he would probably be sentenced to three months of forced labor on the highways for concealment of a debt commitment or whatever they might call it. A judge or the chief of police would surely find the right word, and, regardless of what the Indian said or did not say, he had committed a serious breach of the law.

He took off his red woolen sash. His rolled-up white cotton trousers slipped down and he stood naked before Don Sixto. He did not even notice it because sadness and bitterness filled his mouth, his stomach, his soul. Carefully and slowly he unwound the sash, as though through his delay he might protect his hard-earned money which was to give him the possibility of marriage and the prospect of fathering fifteen children. Of course he could not hide a single centavo without Don Sixto noticing it.

Slowly though he moved, he finally unwound his sash completely. To prevent the money from rolling around on the ground, he squatted on his haunches, supporting his arms on his knees. Then he took the silver pesos from the sash and gave them to Don Sixto one by one, thinking as he did so how hard he had worked for each of the pretty coins.

He did not count, but Don Sixto called out the amount as each peso was placed in his hand.

Every time Don Sixto had ten pesos in his hand he emptied the hand by shoving the money into his pants pockets, first into the right, then into the left, then into the right hip pocket, then into the left hip pocket, then again into the right front pocket.

Don Emiliano looked on, silently counting with him. Counting money was more interesting than getting annoyed over the governor's corruption and the unbuilt highway.

Eventually, Don Sixto had seventy pesos in his pockets. He again opened his hand, held it out to Celso, and when he had seven more pesos, he said: "Basta, muchacho. Now I'll give you back four reales. Honesty is the best policy. Not a centavo more would I ever take from a poor Indito than what he really owes me. And now I'm going to write you a receipt. I don't want you to think that I intend to come back a second time to ask for my money. Honesty and decency is the fundamental law of the religion I believe in."

Celso rose from his haunches and stood up.

At this moment a policeman came along, telling Celso to pull up his pants and fasten them carefully or he would be arrested for having committed an immoral act in public. And in this way Celso was jolted back into reality. During the last few minutes he had moved as though in a state of hypnosis.

Don Sixto, having the money and therefore being in good humor, admonished the policeman that everything was in order and that there was no reason to molest the young Indian who, anyway, by now had obeyed the policeman's order.

With a big grin on his lips Don Sixto pulled out of his coat pocket a folded notebook, carefully tore out a leaf and wrote on it a few lines to the effect that he had received from Francisco Flores payment in full for two oxen by collecting the out-standing balance of seventy-six pesos and fifty centavos as of that day. He signed his name with a great flourish, thinking that thus it was safe from imitation by any impostor.

He handed Don Emiliano the bit of paper together with his pen. "Don Emiliano, will you please sign here as a witness?"

"Sure, nothing easier."

Don Emiliano signed his name even more decoratively than Don Sixto.

"Come along with me," Don Sixto told Celso. "I'll fix it right now with the taxes, so that you'll have a valid receipt for your father."

He left Celso outside, waiting, while he had the employee in the branch office of la Hacienda Federal put on the stamps and cancel them. He then returned with Celso to the plaza, where Don Emiliano was still sitting on the bench, smoking cigarettes and meditating over the deficiencies of a government of which he, to his chagrin, was not a part. Don Sixto sat down by his side and gave Celso the paper.

"Here, you've got your receipt now," he said, "and Don Emiliano is a witness that you've paid me for the oxen. This paper with the stamps on it is now legal. The brand of the oxen has also been noted on it. Don't think that I'm taking money away from you unlawfully. Many others wouldn't be as generous with an Indito as I am. They wouldn't have made you a present of the tax stamps, as I did; anybody not as kind-hearted as I am would've made you pay for those stamps. All right, muchacho, now run along. Give your father this receipt and tell him everything is okay now. Don't you buy any aguar-diente at the last tienda on your way home. And tell your father that if he wants a cow or a mule or the best seed in the state he can get it from me at the cheapest price in the whole comarca."

Celso turned around, intending to retrieve his bananas from

where he had left them on the curb. At the same moment he noticed a dog lifting his hind leg against them. Celso walked over to his spoiled bananas and with the tip of his foot shoved them into the gutter.

2

    With heavy steps Celso walked toward the church
which filled one side of the square. The side entrance to the church was opposite the soldiers' barracks, el
cuartel.

Celso stopped before the little table which served as counter
for a woman who had set up shop inside the church entrance.
He bought two green candles, a little silver star and a small
silver heart. One candle he offered the Holy Virgin for having
protected him on his way, another candle he offered to a statue
which he believed to be San Andrés, the patron saint of his
comarca. He gave the silver star to the female statue of a saint
whose name he did not know, nor did he know why he did this
at all. But the woman who sold it explained to him that offering
it to the image would bring him very good luck. The little silver heart he placed on the balustrade of the main altar in the
hope that during the night the Holy Virgin would descend
from her thick gilt frame and come to pick it up.

When he placed the silver heart on the balustrade he thought
of the girl he wanted to marry.

Not until this moment, and not for a single time during his
dealings with Don Sixto, had he been fully aware of the fact

that he had worked two long years in the coffee plantation for nothing. To get the girl for his wife was now many times further from realization than it had been on the day when he signed up for two years' work on the finca. He was unable to perceive in his mind how it had been possible for him to hand Don Sixto all his money without protesting, without even attempting to run away. Not until now did it dawn upon him that the whole deal might have been a fraud. But he knew Don Sixto and his standing in the community and Celso had an enormous respect for him, a respect which, however, was principally fear. Don Sixto had only to call a policeman and say: "Lock up this Chamula bastard in the calabozo!" and Celso would have been arrested, thrown into jail and kept there until Don Sixto told his compadre, the chief of police: "Now set that pig free!" For Don Sixto was a highly influential citizen of the town, and highly influential citizens have their privileges.

Celso knelt on the stone floor which was thickly strewn with pine needles and prayed: "Ave Maria, Madre de Dios, ora pro nobis." Ten times he repeated it. He did not know what it meant, or what its purpose was, but his mother had said it so often when he accompanied her to church in Jovel that he finally had learned to babble it himself. It was all he knew about praying. And it was all his mother could teach him because she did not know anything else.

Finishing his simple prayer, he joined the tips of his index finger and thumb, touched them to his lips, and kissed his thumb several times. He had complied faithfully with every little detail his mother had told him to observe when he came back from the plantation. He had offered proper thanks for his safe return to the saints in the church in Jovel, the last town before reaching his native village.

He had left his pack in care of the woman from whom he had bought the bananas. He went there, picked up the pack and headed for home.

The last house in the outskirts of the town was a tienda, a small store where an Indian peasant could obtain everything he might need. However, very few wares were for sale. The limited goods stocked on the shaky shelves, dusty and with signs of not having been touched for ages, were not really destined for sale. They were merely a cover to prove to the controlling inspectors that legitimate merchandise actually was offered at the store. Of course every inspector knew that the merchandise was placed there only so that he could swear he had been under the impression that it was a legally established general store. It was not necessary to mention that he had been offered and accepted a so-called mordida, a bribe to make his report in accordance with the wishes of the store owner. Should a complaint ever be filed, which was not likely to happen, the judge, who ate from the same plate as did the inspector, as well as all the other officials, would be of a comprehending nature and benevolent enough not to ask inconvenient questions.

Even had his wares been of good quality, the storekeeper, a gachupín, would not have been able to do much business. Nobody buys his supplies at the last or first house of a town unless he has previously examined prices and values of merchandise in the center of the market place where competition forces the merchants to keep the prices fair.

The business transacted by this storekeeper was simple but lucrative. He sold contraband aguardiente. The profits on untaxed aguardiente are considerably higher than those obtained by selling the taxed kind. The vendor shared with the consumer the money which the government extracted from the distilling and sale of liquors. And as, in this particular case, the vendor was also the manufacturer of the booze, the profits doubled.

The storekeeper had no license for the sale of alcoholic beverages. This would have been bothersome, because it surely would attract inspectors who would find the untaxed stuff and impose a fine of fifty times the tax. Nor did this vendor sell aguardiente in glasses. For that he would have needed an extra license for keeping a bar. Some owners of bars who paid their taxes honestly would have denounced him.

This smart merchant sold the aguardiente by the bottle, yet not in sealed bottles. Patrons had to bring along their own bottles. But if they had no bottle, in that case the bottle was sold also and rebought after it had been emptied. One can sell more per bottle than per glass.

Nobody was allowed to drink inside the store. That was strictly prohibited. The patrons drained their bottles outside, on the road, or back of the store, in the patio.

By the sides of the house, back of the house and along the road which led to the Indian villages, men, women and youths lay in the sun, all dead drunk, many of them in rags, their hair matted and full of lice, the drunken women with their skirts up to their breasts. The drunken men were howling, yelling, swearing, snoring, dancing. A grotesque picture painted by a great artist from hell with sufficient irony to underscore that oily platitude: God made man after his own image.

Every inhabitant of the town, every child knew that at this place moonshine was being sold to Indians. Every fiscal tax inspector knew it. Yet everybody pretended not to know anything. The owner of the prosperous tienda shared his earnings liberally with the tax and alcohol inspectors, with the mayor, with the judge and the chief of police. Therefore, he was powerful and feared all around.

The country was so full of really good and wise laws that you couldn't turn around without stepping into one law and stepping over at least three others. Few countries in the world have a finer constitution and better laws. And one of these really good laws strictly prohibits the sale of hard liquor to Indians. However, all these good laws seemed to have no other purpose but that senadores, diputados, state governors, labor leaders, mayors, secret service men, judges, chiefs of police, jail wardens and all those fortunate enough to grab some public office could by all imaginable means of extortion enrich themselves faster than the luckiest gambler at the stock exchange.

On his way home Celso arrived at this store which, as it was only an adobe hut, without windows and roofed with clapboards, would have seemed to an American tourist as innocent as great grandmother's little candy store in Sandy Creek.

For a while he sat down on the grassy curb of the dusty dirt road, resting against his pack. His idea had been to buy several little things in Jovel to take home with him as presents: new huaraches for his father, a bright red woolen ribbon for his mother to be braided into her thick hair and a glittering pearl necklace for his girl.

Now he was coming home without any gifts. His eyes fell upon drunken men and women who were groaning like lost cattle and lying around on the bare ground, dead to the world, and who had thrown away the last remnants of human dignity which they had preserved until then in spite of their poverty.

Celso returned, not only without presents, but also without any money for his marriage. To rich Don Sixto seventy-six pesos and fifty centavos meant no more than a snap of his fingers. He gambled away twice as much in two hours at roulette at the plaza or playing dice or dominos in the cantina. To Celso these same seventy-six pesos meant fifteen children and everything he needed to build up a world of his own and give meaning to his life.

Leaving his pack outside he entered the store where he pointed to a red woolen ribbon that hung by a thread from a peg. It was covered with dust to such a degree that its color appeared to be grey. The storekeeper had never for a moment thought of selling this ribbon, or for that matter anything else exposed in his store. It was, therefore, a matter of complete indifference to him whether the wares were covered with dust or faded or nibbled at by rats.

In utter boredom he picked his teeth, lazily turned around in such a way as not to lose for an instant the comfortable support of the counter as an armrest, dimly looked at the ribbon, turned his eyes back just as lazily, pulled down one corner of his mouth, winked with one eye and said: "Bueno, joven, where are you from? Oh, well, from Ishtacolcot. You don't look like a Chamula. Must have come from the monterías, eh? Am I right, am I?"

"How much for that ribbon?" Celso asked again.

"Well, now look! Look there," said the gachupín highly astonished. "Seems you got stout and fat. Bien gordo, I'd say. Plenty of time to take it easy. Ishtacolcot won't run away. Ain't you going to have a drink? Have it on me."

Celso turned around, ready to leave.

"Hey, you," the merchant yelled, slightly disturbed in his laziness, "don't run away. You can have the ribbon. It will cost you eight reales."

The price in town would have been two reales.

Celso opened his sash a bit. No need to take it off again to reach the remains of his fortune. From a pleat of his untwisted sash he took the money that remained and counted it. When he noticed that the storekeeper was watching him, he became distrustful and turned around. He still had forty-seven centavos left.

"Can you let me have the ribbon for forty-seven fierros?" he asked. This was still nearly twice the money at which he could have had the ribbon in town.

"No, that I cannot do by the Santísima and by San José, I can't let you have it for that price. I'd go broke." The toothpick in the storekeeper's mouth wandered by itself from one corner to the other. Placing his fat hands on the counter he said: "I'll tell you what I'll do for you. A pint bottle costs fifty centavos. For you, I'll let it go for forty-seven. So you see that if I can sell something for less I'm willing to do it to please my customers."

Celso arrived at home without gifts, without money for his marriage and without his pack, which he had lost somewhere along the road. He stumbled into the house and into the lap of his mother who was sitting on her haunches on the earthen floor in front of the fire, cooking the evening meal.

3

On the following day, when it was possible to talk to Celso again as a human being, his father asked him what had become of the money earned during the two years.

"Don Sixto took it away from me."

"That is right," said the father, "that I owe Don Sixto the money for the two oxen. But there's no truth about my promising him the balance for the oxen from your wages. We had agreed that I was going to discuss the purchase with you, when you came home from the coffee finca, because you were to see and appraise the oxen first. I was going to give you those oxen when your first child was born. And if you did not like the oxen, I was free to return them to Don Sixto and he would have given me back what payment I had made, or credit it to my account for a mule. We had agreed that I was to give Don Sixto six pesos every two months until the oxen were paid for in full, and that we would legalize the bill of sale with the authorities in Jovel after you returned. That was the agreement."

Here, in his father's house, where under the shade of the palm-thatched roof his mother, squatting before the metate, was grinding the masa for the noon meal, everything seemed so simple. Everything sounded so clear and without double meaning here in his village, surrounded by a thick double fence of magueyes, where dogs barked out of boredom, where donkeys brayed lazily, where turkeys gobbled, chickens cackled, children shouted and where everything was peaceful, harmonious and in perfect accord with the surroundings—all was downright straightforward, pure, sincere, guileless, direct.

How different words had sounded in the gruff mouth of Don Sixto, who did not discuss, but gave short orders instead. All had been utterly different at the plaza in Jovel, with Celso standing in front of the two haughty caballeros sitting on the bench, and with his back to the menacing, massive building with the large, almost threatening letters *Presidencia Municipal*, and in thick black letters over the doors, which seemed like entrances to so many caves, *Juez Penal, Tesorería, Jefe de Policía, Cárcel*. What could Celso do under these oppressive influences and caught in such surroundings? He would have handed over all his money even if Don Sixto had handled the deal with less astuteness. Neither Celso nor his father thought of going to Jovel and demanding their money back from Don Sixto. It would have been in vain. And if they were to get excited and give Don Sixto just one single nasty word, both would be thrown in jail. Francisco Flores, father of Celso, had two oxen, and Don Sixto, who had sold him the two oxen, had duly received the money and extended a legally valid receipt. He had even been liberal enough to pay for the tax stamps out of his pocket. It would have taken days for Celso and his father with their limited knowledge of Spanish to make the authorities understand that some shady action had crept into the deal, which, for Celso, had shattered more future dreams than could ever be made good by the best oxen in the world and the most perfect, most legal, tax-stamped receipt.

Later the same day Celso went to search for his pack. He

found it. Since only Indians came along the way he had come, nobody had touched his belongings.

He was ashamed to look up his girl.

But when he had been home for more than a week, working every day with his father in the milpa, the cornfield, training the young oxen how to pull the plow and had been seen by all the people in the village, one afternoon, shortly before sundown, the father of the girl came to Francisco Flores' jacal.

Behind the father, at a certain distance, the daughter walked along.

The girl's father, Manuel Laso, entered the yard, greeted them with a few short words and sat down on a low bench.

The girl remained outside, close to the fence. She was barefooted, wore the usual rough black woolen skirt reaching down to her knees, and she was adorned with a necklace of green glass beads. Her thick black hair was in plaits interwoven with a red woolen ribbon and neatly set up on top of her head in the form of a crown. She held her hands crossed over her bosom and hid her face in them. But she was looking interestedly through her fingers and everybody could see, and obviously was meant to see, that nothing of what took place in the hut or in the yard escaped her.

Celso's mother got up from the fire, came out of the hut, made a short curtsy before the guest, held the tips of her fingers out to him, which he touched lightly, and then walked up to the fence to invite the girl to come in.

As though she had committed some serious offense the girl passed like a shadow by the side of the woman and disappeared into the hut, where she sat down near the fire next to the woman and both began to chat.

Celso had been working back of the house, hacking out a harness for the oxen.

He now came into the front yard and greeted the girl's father as casually as if it did not matter to him whether he was there or not. He did not bother to greet the girl. He did not even look at her and he avoided entering the hut. However he could not stand it for long. He stepped to the door of the hut and asked his mother whether she had seen his knife. He, of course, knew where it was. It had been stuck into a pole of the hut, and to get it, he had to cross the whole floor. He went to the pole with straight eyes, never glancing at the girl who was squatting on her haunches.

At the moment he entered, the girl hid her face in the high front part of her skirt. But sideways and from underneath she followed the youth's every movement. Though she had little to say in the selection of her husband, because this was a matter of the two fathers and of the marriageable young man, she was nevertheless curious to get a good look at the man who, for the last two years, had been promised to her. She was now fifteen years old and it was time for her and for her parents to think seriously of the future. At twenty-one she would be a dust-covered, hopeless old maid. At that age only by being a widow would she have a chance to get a mate.

When Celso came out of the hut Manuel Laso shouted at him across the yard: "Hey, you, muchacho, why haven't you come over to me to say good day and how do you do? I've been expecting you."

"I haven't had the time, Don Manuel. Now since we have got the young oxen I want to break them in for my father before I leave again."

"Before you leave again?" asked Manuel Laso.

"Leave again for where, boy?" asked Celso's father. It had come to him just as unexpectedly as it had to Manuel Laso.

"To earn the money for my marriage," said Celso, as though he was surprised that they did not know it already.

Manuel Laso frowned and grumbled: "I thought you'd brought the money for getting married from the cafetal. You've been working hard there for two years, I understand."

"But, Don Manuel, I haven't got the money and that's why I've got to leave again."

Celso did not mention that he had paid the money for the oxen. Nor did his father disclose it. It was against certain unwritten rules. What had become of the money was actually of no consequence. All that mattered was that Celso produce the various presents the girl's father had to be given before he would agree to accept Celso as his son-in-law. It was a matter of principle. More likely than not Manuel Laso had an idea that the money in question might have something to do with Francisco Flores' recently acquired oxen. But it was not his business to stick his nose into the matter. Not in the least did it alter the plain fact that Celso did not have the money he needed to pay the girl's father according to established custom.

Francisco Flores said: "I've promised my son Celso that team of oxen when his first child is born. But you know, Don Manuel, I'd be quite willing to give Celso the team right now."

"The team of oxen is not important in the deal which I have with Celso, Don Pancho," replied Manuel Laso. "You told me some time ago that you would give Celso those oxen when he was blessed with his first child. I must say that is very good of you. But it has nothing to do with my deal which I have with Celso. He must earn the money for his marriage by himself and without your help. I must know if that vagabond is capable of earning money. You can't expect me to give my daughter to a golfo, to a good-for-nothing, unable to earn money when it's needed. Celso is all right with me, and the chamaca has told my old woman that Celso is quite all right with her also. But that won't last long. What counts in the long run is the capacity to work and to make ends meet. So, now, I'll say my last word in this matter: Celso, you will have to earn the money, you and not your father. You it is who wants my daughter, not your father. I'll give you another two years. That girl of mine could have any boy if I consented. But I'd like to have you for a son, and the chamaca likes you. And so I'll grant you another two years to get the money. But more than two years my daughter can't wait. She's too old for that."

Manuel Laso got up, held out his hand to Francisco Flores and called toward the door of the hut: "I'm leaving."

Celso's mother came to the door and said: "Adiosito, Don Manuel."

"Hasta luego," replied Don Manuel, "until later."

He went on his way.

Like a scared little dog the girl approached Francisco Flores, her father-in-law to be, bowed and kissed his hand.

He placed his other hand on the girl's head and said: "Vete con Dios, God be with you, chiquita mía."

Without looking up and with her body bent, in the same attitude in which she had taken leave of Don Francisco, she turned rapidly and ran with fast, short steps after her father. Once outside the fence, she straightened up a bit and glanced over her shoulder into the yard, first covering her face with both hands.

Celso was leaning against one of the poles which supported the overhanging roof of the hut, whittling on a stick. The firm attention he paid the stick in his hand gave the impression that it was a highly important piece of work for the harness of the oxen. However, he really was only whittling idly without any definite idea of embellishing the piece of wood or increasing its usefulness. He did not seem to notice the girl, and her shy look through the fingers of her hand, as if gazing through a lattice window, was the only gesture she made to signify that Celso was, for her, the only man on earth.

Not until, by his estimate, the girl's father was at least two hundred paces away did Celso look up. But his hand continued to whittle on the stick so that, had he noticed that anyone was watching him, he had but to lower his lids to be protected against any suspicion that he wanted only that girl, and none other, to become the mother of his fifteen children.

When still a boy, living permanently in the village, he had occasionally seen the girl rather close: once, when el cura had come to baptize the children in the half-ruined church of the village, and another time, at a wedding, when he had danced four times with her, and now and then when both families had met on the road, returning from the market at Jovel. If he took careful and exact count, all the words exchanged with the girl up to that date would not amount to more than twenty.

Even at the dance he had merely approached her and, as was the custom, thrown his red bandanna into her lap to indicate that he asked for the honor of dancing with her. He would not have known what to say to her. That it was hot or cold, that it was going to rain or that they were thirsty, such silly little things the girl knew by herself. So why ask about it? Even to say "thank you" or "how are you?" would have sounded so ridiculous that the village might have gossiped about it for months. And much less was it necessary for him to tell her that he was fond of her. If she did not know that by herself then she was not to be considered as a possible mother of his fifteen children. Whether she wanted to marry or not was not a matter between her and him, but solely a matter between him and her father. She could say "no" to any deal concerted by the two men. That was her right. But then any other boy in the village was of the same standing. Neither she nor any female of her tribe had been educated to see or feel a particular difference between one man and another. What little distinction there might exist between one marriageable man and another was to be appraised by her father and not by her.

These distinctions consisted in that one man was a drunkard, the other a moderate drinker and the third a youth who would not even touch aguardiente. Other differences might be that, according to the judgment of the girl's father, one man might not know how to work well and constantly, while the other was capable, experienced and hard working. The most important difference, and again in the judgment of her father, lay in the fact that one youngster might not seem capable of helping his wife to ten children, while the other gave the father the impression that he might easily produce twenty children and feed them. Sentiment does not count for much in the marriage of an Indian peasant. What counts is down-to-earth reality.

Yet, from the day when Celso had discussed with the girl's father the compensation for the marriage, the girl had commenced to accustom herself to the idea that Celso, and no other man under the sun, had been destined for her through all eternity. And Celso, had he been able to express it poetically, would most likely have affirmed that the girl had been destined for him by fate since the creation of the world as the one and only woman. They would marry, without the benefit of the church or of the civil judge, merely by the agreement of both parents. Whether the couple, once married for thirty years, was happy or not none would know. The happiness of marriage was something beyond the scope of their sentiments. They would have children, half of them dead, the other alive, some of them married. They would live by constant hard work, for the very moment they stopped working, even if only for two months, there would be no corn and no beans to eat.

They would live together in peace. Beginning with the day they married the woman would obey the husband more than she would obey God, of whom she had only a very vague conception anyhow. What her husband said and ordered was an unalterable law for her and all her children, whether they still lived under his roof or had homes of their own. Just as a good Catholic would not think of criticizing a command given by the Pope or of examining his right to create new dogmas, thus the woman would never dream of criticizing a decision or an order of her man. They both discussed how, when, where and at what price they were going to sell their surplus of corn, wool, goats or skins. If they agreed, good. If they didn't agree, he had the last word. If, after some time had passed, it turned out that her judgment had proven better than his, she would not puff up or throw it in his face any more than a pious human being would grumble when God, instead of sending rain, lets everything perish by a long drought.

4

 Celso packed his few belongings and, one morning at three o'clock, he was again on the road to Jovel.

Arriving in town, he bought five centavos worth of raw tobacco leaves in a store at the Zócalo. His mother had staked him to a tostón, that is, half a peso, for his trip to town. Now he was sitting on the curb outside the store, rolling himself some cigars.

Inside the store a caballero was discussing with the storekeeper the possibilities of sending a thick envelope with documents and letters to the montería Agua Azul. For several days he had been looking for arrieros who might be going that way. The arrieros were the mule drivers who led pack trains to the faraway districts of the state where there were no roads for vehicles. As it turned out there were no arrieros right now taking a caravan to Agua Azul or a camp nearby. Perhaps in two or three months, when the Turk would take his merchandise to the monterías, there might be a chance to deliver the envelope. But most certainly it would not be today or within the next two or three weeks.

The caballero needed someone very urgently to take the important documents to that montería. But no messenger would go alone. Everyone was afraid of the long march through the jungle, which would take at least ten days, to which the trip back had to be added. From Jovel to the last village before entering the jungle it was six days. Counting the necessary rest days, the round trip would require some forty days of the bearer's time. Naturally he would ask to be paid for forty days. This had to be increased by the hire of his horse and the pack mule to carry the provisions needed for the trip. Occasionally the mule was interchanged for the horse, so as not to wear out the animals. A horse or a mule that gets too tired in the jungle simply lies down, refuses to eat and may easily die of despair. Besides, being afraid to go alone, whoever went demanded a companion. Such a demand was not unreasonable. But that boy, too, had to have a horse and had to be paid for forty days.

Simply to stick a ten-centavo stamp on the letter, throw it into the nearest letter box, and then run away would not have helped the caballero much. The letter would have been returned to him with the note "No hay correos," that is, "No postal communications."

"Listen, Don Apolinar," the storekeeper said. "Why don't you send the letter with a Chamula Indian? They don't need horses. They run like the devil after a soul. Once they are on the run, two horses won't catch them."

"Now, there's an idea worth considering," said Don Apolinar.

"Nothing to consider," replied the storekeeper. "Just ask that Chamula over there, sitting on the curb and rolling his cigars. I can vouch for him. I know him and his father. He is from Ishtacolcot."

Originally Celso, like all of his tribe, had only spoken Tsotsil, his mother tongue. But even before going to work at the coffee fincas, he had begun to learn Spanish while working for some months in the sawmill of Don Prisciliano for two reales, twenty-five centavos a day. In the coffee fincas, where he met so many workers speaking four different Indian languages that Spanish was a necessity for them to understand one another, he had perfected himself in this language as much as it was possible for an Indian who had never gone to school.

He heard what the two ladinos were saying, but pretended not to understand Spanish in order to learn exactly what was being discussed, since he had been mentioned.

An Indian who lives in his pueblo is generally slow in understanding such things and even slower in grasping an opportunity to derive some advantage for himself. Yet because of his working at the coffee fincas, where he met not only pure Indians, but also the slimy, shrewd and oily scum of the cities who frequently went to work at the faraway coffee plantations for no other reason than to hide away from the police for a while, Celso had begun to shake off the clumsiness of his thinking process. However, he had not yet succeeded in getting rid of it completely, otherwise he would not have stumbled into Don Sixto's trap so easily, but would have tried to defend himself and waited to see whether he would really be sent to jail if he did not pay Don Sixto. Being afraid of jail was one of the complexes which he had not been able to get rid of. He had seen too often how quickly, and without any real cause, innocent Indians were picked up, dragged to jail and from there driven to road building with no pay.

But what little he had learned at the coffee plantations in the way of seeking an advantage for himself in a given situation now came in very handy.

Without that experience he probably would have jumped up and humbly offered Don Apolinar his services to take the letter to Agua Azul. But he remained sitting, because he had learned that a man who offers himself is worth only half as much as one who is being sought.

Calmly he continued sitting on the curb, slowly and with great care rolling his cigars. And since he acted so innocently the two caballeros discussed the wage for the carrier without restraint.

"Do you think that stinker would do it for two reales a day?" asked Don Apolinar.

"He can do it in thirty days and that would be—let's see—sixty reales, well, seven pesos and fifty centavos," replied the merchant.

"Hey, listen, you, Chamula!" shouted Don Apolinar.

Celso got up. He came with the shy and fearful gesture of the simple Indian who is unexpectedly called by a ladino and who does not know what to expect, whether a kick in the behind, or jail, or a cigarette or a glass of aguardiente, or some unpaid service, or showing his vaccination marks, or giving his name or information about how many sheep he keeps at home.

However, for the first time in his life, Celso acted with well-studied hypocrisy. Faked was the fearful and shy gesture with which he approached Don Apolinar. He was aware that neither the chief of police, nor the jefe político nor even the governor himself had anything to say in this deal. Any authority could command him to take the envelope to the montería without any payment whatsoever, even without compensation for his food. But if it was stolen from him while he was asleep, or if the envelope unwound accidentally from his woolen sash and got lost in the jungle, or if it dissolved into pulp while he was swimming through a river, not even the death penalty for him could replace the important documents and bank notes. And since the possibilities of losing the envelope or of its turning into pulp because of constant rain were so numerous, nobody could prove whether he had or had not handled it with due care or perhaps lost it intentionally to revenge himself for the unpaid labor forced upon him.

This envelope with its very important documents was a highly confidential matter which could only be handled voluntarily and in good faith to please the man interested in the safe arrival of the letter. He, therefore, feigned a shy gesture so as not to give away the fact that, in this case, he was looking out for his own advantage.

While sitting on the curb listening to them talk about the envelope and of the difficulties of its transportation, he had begun, without any outward sign, to muse over a plan. And a minute later he knew that taking this important letter to the montería was a stroke of luck which had fallen upon him in his present situation.

His first intention had been to return to a coffee finca, although he was fed up with the work and would have liked to find something else. But when he learned that there were no recruiting agents in town and that no demand for labor at the cafetales existed, he began to think of the monterías as the only remaining solution. It was very hard work, work that could be called murderous. But he was not afraid of hard work. What he wanted was to avoid the high expenses connected with obtaining work in a montería. The agents demanded between twenty-five and fifty pesos commission for recruiting. The labor contract stipulated another twenty-five pesos tax to be paid to the mayor in Hucutsin. The march, or rather the food consumed on the march, was on his own account. All this amounted to more than three months' wages, solely as expenses for the right to work.

And now, while he was meditating about his desperate situation, the envelope fell right into his lap. The march would be paid for. He would get to a montería. There was a perpetual and steady demand for workers in the monterías. He would not pay any commission to an agent, nor would he have to pay twenty-five pesos tax in Hucutsin. He would work in the montería without a contract and so be free to leave when he wanted to and when he thought that he had earned the money needed for his marriage.

5

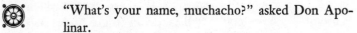"What's your name, muchacho?" asked Don Apolinar.

"Celso, Celso Flores, a sus órdenes, patroncito."

Although Don Apolinar knew it, since the merchant had just told him, he still demanded: "And where do you come from?"

"Ishtacolcot, patroncito."

"That's some leguas beyond la villa de Chamula?"

"Sí, señor, más o menos dos leguas."

"That means about six miles."

"So I think, patroncito."

"Do you know the way to the monterías? To any montería in the region of the Ushumahcintla River?"

"No, patroncito."

Don Apolinar began to explain the road. He took a piece of wrapping paper lying on the counter and drew a line on it. Since Celso did not know how to read, Don Apolinar drew little squares wherever there was a village or a hamlet. Furthermore, for each place he drew a certain figure, consisting of a special landmark, such as church or a high, oddly formed rock or a big tree or the location of the cemetery. Thus the road became as clear to Celso's comprehension as a railroad timetable to a traveling salesman. In this way Don Apolinar drew the exceedingly difficult road which he himself had covered several times as far as the last settlement at the edge of the great jungle. From there on it was not so easy to sketch the road on paper as the road was actually only a mere path. All he could tell Celso was to spend the night in the last settlement and there obtain from the settlers a detailed description of the way through the jungle. In the same settlement he would also have to buy all the food he needed on his march through the jungle, because once in the jungle there would be no stores, no huts, no human beings. The way through the jungle would require from nine to twelve days, depending on the speed of the runner.

"So here you see, joven, how the road worms along and more or less how long it will take you to get to Agua Azul," said Don Apolinar. "And now we shall discuss your pay. You can very well make the entire trip in thirty days, a fortnight to get there, and a fortnight back. I shall give you two reales for every day. That would be a total of seven pesos and fifty centavos, and if you handle the matter well I shall add another eight reales as a special bonus."

Celso listened without nodding his head, without arguing, without showing by a single expression on his face that he had even understood what had been said to him. Once he had seen where and how his advantage would come in, he thought he might just as well continue, otherwise his plan would be of no use. While Don Apolinar was talking, it occurred to Celso that he might perhaps get back from Don Apolinar at least some part of what Don Sixto had taken away from him. Don Apolinar and Don Sixto both were ladinos and they could straighten out their accounts between them. Without knowing the economic circumstances and interlacing of the business deals made by the ladinos among themselves, Celso had in his mind a faint idea that if one ladino lost something in favor of another one, he would try to recover it from a third ladino, and that from those intricate and intermingled dealings arose all the quarrels and discussions and shootings with which the ladinos seemed to fill the better part of their lives. Consequently, if he, Celso, made Don Apolinar pay him well, the latter would get it back from some other ladino until, finally, the money that now had to be paid by Don Apolinar to Celso would be extracted from the pockets of Don Sixto.

With a shy, servile and stupid face, Celso said: "With your kind permission, patroncito, I don't believe that I can go. It's really too far. I'm afraid of the jungle. It's full of Caribes, those savages who steal women and kill all Indians who are not Caribes and can't speak their language."

"The Caribes are kind and peaceful people and they won't do you any harm as long as you don't bother them."

"But they use poisoned arrows when anybody crosses their paths or comes near their huts."

"That's fairy tales, old women's talk."

"But I'm still afraid," repeated Celso. "There are many tigers and pumas and poisonous snakes in the jungle and I have no gun to defend myself."

"But you have your machete," argued Don Apolinar.

"True, I have one, patroncito," said Celso miserably, as if somebody expected him to go on an elephant hunt with nothing but a dull fishhook on a piece of thread.

"Sometimes a machete is worth two good guns," the storekeeper said, calming Celso. "There are times a gun won't fire just when a tiger is ready to jump, and then what?"

"Bueno, right now I wouldn't know what to do in that case," said Celso. "I would have to see first how things stand and how big the tiger is."

Don Apolinar and the merchant both laughed and felt rich and important before the innocence and stupidity of the Chamula boy.

"How about a drink, muchacho?" asked Don Apolinar invitingly. He had a bottle of fine cognac in front of him and was ready to serve a glass. But in that same instant he realized that a small glass of cognac was sixty centavos, while a big glass of native mezcal could be had for five. He was just going to ask the storekeeper for the aguardiente bottle, but the man had had the idea at the same time as Don Apolinar. Not for nothing were they both ladinos, and both had come from the same school where the boy calls the Indian, even if he is ninety years old, "tú" and "oye tú, ven acá," while the old Indian has to call the ladino boy, even if he can't wipe his nose by himself, "usted" and "don," if he wants to enjoy the right to sit on the doorstep of the house and wait, perhaps the entire afternoon, until the lady of the house finally remembers to pay the Indian the six centavos for the firewood which he carried to the house and which he had to drag along for perhaps ten miles to earn.

As the abarrotero and Don Apolinar had grown up in the same social stratum the merchant had the stone jug with the mezcal already in his hand.

But very politely Celso said: "Mil gracias, patroncito, no tomo, I don't drink."

"Bueno, bueno," said Don Apolinar and the storekeeper placed the stone jug back on the shelf.

Don Apolinar now added in a firm voice: "Pues, so you'll go, muchacho."

"Muy lejos, demasiado lejos el camino," answered Celso, defending himself very astutely. In truth, he now started to attack: "It is too far, much too far. And by far too dangerous."

"I'll tell you something, muchacho, I'll give you three reales per day, three reales, thirty-seven centavos for each day."

"And the food, patroncito? Where am I going to get my food?"

"Well, the food, of course, you'll have to buy on the way."

"With the three reales, patroncito? How can I do that?"

"It won't cost you more than half a real or perhaps even only a quinto."

"But then I won't have left three reales per day for doing the job, patroncito, con su permiso."

Celso spoke ever more humbly, more submissively, more politely. He seemed to get more stupid by the minute and to understand less and less. The sliest recruiting agent would not have discovered that the ladino was not playing with the Indian but the Indian with the ladino. The game was all the more alluring as neither Don Apolinar nor the storekeeper, both believing themselves so far superior, had the slightest inkling that Celso was just pulling their legs. The humbler, the more submissive, the more frightened Celso seemed, the more godlike the two caballeros felt, and the more careless and lenient Don Apolinar became in his dealings with Celso.

When Don Apolinar offered twenty-five centavos he had supposed, without thinking, that the matter of food was none of his affair. Celso, seemingly getting every minute more and more stupid, had not mentioned the food when the twenty-five centavos were discussed. He only brought the subject of food into the discussion when the wages had already been raised to three reales. Three reales was the pay; and owing to the manner in which it had now been brought into the deal the food, of course, could no longer be deducted from the wages.

"Well, my last word, muchacho, I'll give you four reales per day," said Don Apolinar in a tone which indicated that the deal had now finally been closed.

"But, patroncito, señorito, my kind master and little father, with your so very kind permission, and I hope you'll forgive me, but I can't make that trip in a fortnight. Not even a horse can make that road in a fortnight." Celso was almost in tears now, and he said it in such a way as if neither he nor the horse were guilty of the length of time but that it was strictly the road's fault.

Don Apolinar, bored by the long negotiations, did not quite listen to what Celso was saying. He remembered that barely a quarter of an hour ago there had been talk of forty days, twenty to go, twenty to return, and that in the case of having to send a mounted carrier, perhaps even with a companion, the letter would have been very expensive. Now, when mentally comparing the amounts, he found the Indian so cheap that he felt an inclination to be liberal. This inclination, however, was immediately mixed with the commercial thought that if he showed himself generous toward Celso, the boy would be in a good humor. Good humor and a willing disposition on behalf of the runner were essential, so that the Indian would not become discouraged along the road and simply come back, return the undelivered letter and renounce all compensation.

"True. The road is long, you are right there, muchacho," Don Apolinar said. "The best I can do, and I'll do it only for you, just for you, because you seem honest, well, I'll pay you, for thirty-five days, four reales every day. If you can deliver the letter within a fortnight, you'll get an extra bonus of two pesos. I'll write that in a special letter to Don Eduardo, who is the señor gerente of the montería. And that letter you deliver to Don Eduardo only in person."

Don Apolinar stopped, because it suddenly struck him that he was now paying Celso more than twice as much as he originally had calculated. He wanted to get some of that back. But since he couldn't do it by lowering the wages, which probably would have ruined the whole deal, he did it by increasing the job demanded. Thus his disturbed economic balance was restored and there was no need to write off the day as a loss.

When he mentioned Don Eduardo, he suddenly remembered that Don Eduardo had asked him for quinine, so very badly needed to get the fever-stricken boys up and back to work.

"Of course, it's not only the papers you've got to take to Agua Azul," he told Celso casually, as if during the whole time far more than just the papers had been discussed. The envelope was thick and heavy, and it constituted sufficient weight for anyone who had to go on foot, climbing over high mountains, swimming across rivers, wading through swamps, cutting his way here and there through the thickets in the jungle, if one considers that the runner also had to carry along enough food for ten days, a tin kettle, a tin pot, a frying pan, a mat and mosquito netting. A little package which, in the morning, weighs ten pounds, will at two in the afternoon weigh thirty pounds on the back of a runner who trots over the burning sand under the tropical sun, half dying of thirst. A soldier on a long march across the Texas plains with full military pack knows well how much an extra pair of boots can weigh on a hot August afternoon after a march of twenty miles, and what difference it can make when he doesn't have to carry his rifle on his shoulder.

"No, it isn't just the papers. This of course you know, Celso Flores. I wouldn't send a strong young man like you just with papers. You understand that, don't you?"

"No lo sé, patroncito," said Celso, shrugging his shoulders, "I wouldn't know."

He began to realize that now it was he, Celso, who was being played with.

"The weight of the letters is hardly enough to even talk about," Don Apolinar said. "You'll have to take along another little package, which I'll get for you at once. Just wait here, I'll step around to the botica, practically next door. Or better still, you come along with me. No, leave your pack here in the store. Don Pedro will see that nobody steals it. Anyway, nothing is ever stolen around here. Everyone in this town is honest. You know that."

Don Apolinar went to the botica and purchased ten pounds of quinine and one thousand gelatine capsules to be filled. The boticario wrapped it all carefully into paper which he claimed was almost waterproof. Then he packed everything in a box. Since he did not find one of the proper size, the box was much larger than necessary. But he told Don Apolinar: "It doesn't matter to the Chamula whether it's a half a yard too long or weighs a few pounds extra. He won't even feel it. They're used to carrying heavy packs."

Don Apolinar and Celso returned to the store.

Leaning over the counter, Don Apolinar wrote a special letter to Don Eduardo in which he told him what Celso was carrying. He wrapped the bulky main letter and the special letter together in thick wrapping paper, securing it with a tough string, and gave Celso the package.

"Where you carry this package of letters is none of my concern. But I can tell you one thing—don't you dare to lose this parcel, or leave it somewhere. And don't let it be stolen while you are asleep. Make sure it doesn't fall in a river where it would float away. If you lose it, juro por Jesucristo, I'll have you locked up in jail for twenty-one years, or better still I'll recommend that you be shot and hanged—anything to make sure you get the maximum punishment. I don't know yet what will be done to you. Perhaps the soldiers will be ordered to chop off your head if you lose the letters."

"Perhaps the soldiers will really do that, patroncito, if I lose the letters."

"I'm glad you realize that. And now see here, if you deliver the package in good share to Don Eduardo he'll pay you the balance which is"—Don Apolinar counted rapidly in his head—"yes, the balance Don Eduardo will pay you is exactly twelve pesos and fifty centavos, considering that I'll give you five pesos in advance. If you deliver the letters in less than fifteen days Don Eduardo will pay you two pesos extra as reward. I've said so in my letter to Don Eduardo."

"Gracias, patroncito. I'm sure Don Eduardo will pay me."

Celso took the parcel with the letters and documents and

shoved it beneath his jorongo into his shirt as carelessly as if it had been just a package of newspapers.

He knew exactly what he was doing. Someone out on the plaza might watch the whole scene. And if Celso treated the parcel of letters as Don Apolinar had expected him to treat it, that is, very cautiously, the one who was spying might think that the package contained lots of money. Celso would be followed along the road and be killed somewhere for the valuable package. Once Celso arrived at a place where he was perfectly sure that nobody could see him, he would hide the package where it was to remain throughout the march.

As was the custom with his tribesmen, he carried his traveling pack in a net. The net had been manufactured at home from strong raw fiber string. It could be opened wide enough to stuff the meat of a whole ox into it, and it could look so shrunken that one would think that not even a newborn calf could be fitted into it.

He opened the net and stowed the box with the quinine among his own belongings. Then he arranged the pack so that the box would not hit against his back.

Now he looked up.

Don Apolinar, seated on a bench in the store and smoking a cigar, had been watching Celso's every move.

He now took five pesos out of his pocket and told the merchant: "Don Pedro, change me five pesos in bronze and silver, five-, ten- and twenty-centavo pieces. The muchacho has no use for large coins along the road, because nobody can give him change."

"I can change two pesos fifty centavos in small coins," said the merchant. "The remaining two pesos and fifty centavos he can easily take along in fifty-centavo pieces. The first four days he'll pass through villages and fincas where he can get change for fifty centavos."

"Gracias, Don Pedro."

"No hay porqué, don't mention it," replied the storekeeper.

"Bueno, Celso," said Don Apolinar, "there you have five pesos, that is, forty reales as an advance on your pay. Don Eduardo will pay you the rest. Now, tomorrow morning early, muy tempranito, and I mean very early, before the sun rises, you'll be on your way."

"Con su permiso, patroncito," Celso interrupted, "with your permission, I'd rather start right now. I'll only buy salt, chile, tortillas, some coffee, piloncillo and green leaves. In a minute I'll be on my way."

"Better, much better." Don Apolinar nodded. "I can see that you're after that two pesos reward. Bueno, off with you and on the run."

Don Apolinar did not offer him his hand. With a fatherly gesture he patted him on the shoulder.

Celso lifted his pack. Then he bowed halfway down and pushed the thumbs of both hands under the front band, to adjust the supporting strap on his forehead so that it wouldn't exert uncomfortable pressure. Now he rose and turned around, ready to go.

Don Apolinar, without stirring from the bench, said: "Buena suerte, good luck on the way."

"Gracias, patroncito, me voy, I'm going," replied Celso and rapidly left the store.

6

 The speed with which Celso went on his way was not caused by his worry about the letters. He could easily have waited until the following morning. But that was exactly what he wanted to avoid.

As Don Apolinar had said, it was not likely that there would be any caravan to the monterías in the next two or even four months. But one could never tell. It might just as well happen that within the next six hours a small patache or even a caravan might arrive in town on its way to the monterías. In that case, Don Apolinar would call Celso, take back the letters and the box, give him twenty centavos for his trouble and entrust the letters and the box to an arriero of the caravan. The arriero would receive a tip of three pesos which he would consider a welcome present, since he had to go to the monterías anyway, and the letters as well as the box would not make the slightest difference to the caravan.

But once Celso had an advantage of two hours in leaving town, Don Apolinar might send the fastest horse after him but it would not be able to catch up with him. Don Apolinar could not send his horseman too far, because that would be expensive. Celso wanted badly to go to the monterías and earn a handsome sum on top of it.

He hurried to get out of town. Nobody knew for certain whether or not he would take the way which Don Apolinar had outlined for him. Along that route a horseman sent after him would discover him soon enough. So Celso took a trail of his own. He had to get safely to the last settlement at the edge of the jungle, to follow from there the only open trail to the monterías. But which way he got to that settlement was his own affair. After all, he was perfectly capable of getting to the settlement without Don Apolinar's penciled sketch.

But no caravan of Syrian or Lebanese peddlers arrived in Jovel on its way to the monterías. And so no mounted messenger was sent after Celso to call him back.

The nearer Celso came to the jungle, the more he realized the difficulties and dangers awaiting him. Because this jungle was quite different from the jungles where he had planted coffee and cleaned weeds from around the coffee trees. Those had been cultivated jungles, with clear and cleaned paths.

When Don Apolinar had talked about the jungle, Celso had thought of the cultivated jungles in the cafetales. He imagined the great jungle as having a slightly thicker overgrowth and greater distances from one established finca to the next, but he still retained the idea that other human faces, voices and actions would be within easy reach.

Yet along his march to the last settlement he had met Indians who knew "la selva grande" and several of them had made the trip to one or another of the various monterías. While passing the night in the huts of Indian peasants, he heard from experienced men all sort of details about the march through the big jungle.

Everyone told him: "You can't make that march alone. Nobody can make it alone. That's the reason why the monterías are so sure of their workers, once they are there." And every other advisor set forth different reasons why a single individual, even though an Indian, could not make the trip by himself.

People who seemed to have his good in mind warned him very seriously against undertaking the march, because it was certain that he would perish in the jungle and his body, perhaps still partly alive, would be eaten by wild beasts, buzzards and ferocious ants.

He had accepted the commission to deliver the letters and the little box to the montería Agua Azul. But to nobody, not even to his own tribesmen whom he met, did he mention the letters. He never spoke of anything but the box with medicine which he had to take to the monterías for the sick people there. He knew nobody would ever steal medicine. If the sick people died because of lack of medicine they would surely, in the form of evil spirits, make life in this world hellishly disagreeable for the thief.

All along the way the people whom he consulted told him the most terrifying stories about the jungle. These people, however, had never been in the jungle themselves; they had not even approached the thicket at the outer edges. All of them recounted merely what others had seen or lived through.

But the various stories related to Celso all contributed, without exception, to inspire in him a terrific fear of the vast jungle. Nobody of course had any definite intention of making Celso desist from his task. Nobody really cared whether Celso perished in the jungle or not. The narrations were made mostly to enjoy the changing expressions of an interested listener, to pass the time away and to get excited over one's own story. Ghost stories, tales of spooks, are not told at night to make someone desist from crossing the cemetery if that is his road home. They are told to spend a pleasant evening by watching with delight the terror-stricken faces of one's audience.

Now a march through the jungle is by no means a holiday hike. The facts came very close to the terrifying narrations of its terrors. Most people with whom Celso came in touch on the road, or in whose huts he spent the nights, were Indians and they were not in the habit of highly exaggerating certain tasks which, in themselves, were natural and which had to be done anyway. Some admitted it might be possible to make the trip alone, but that the difficulties were so considerable and the chances of getting through so slim that it would be far more prudent not to attempt the trip unaccompanied.

Filled up to his scalp with stories, opinions and good advice, Celso arrived at the last settlement. During the second half of the last day he had already been able to obtain an impression of what awaited him. The settlement was located about half a day's march into the jungle, and this part of the road marked a transition from one type of landscape to another. Here and there one saw enough jungle to indicate what the genuine jungle would be like. During the last half day's trip, Celso had not met a single human being, but now and then he had found the footprints of several very large tigers, and on a stout branch of a tree he had seen a large wildcat.

Shortly before noon, he passed through the last hamlet on his march. It was a hamlet composed of only five huts and one adobe house. Right in back of the hamlet Celso waded across a wide river, the water of which reached no higher than a few inches above his knees.

On the opposite side of the river the jungle came into sight. At the beginning it was open and clear, like overgrown land that had been cultivated some fifty years ago and then abandoned. Slowly but definitely noticeably, it grew ever thicker, darker, more imposing and more menacing the farther Celso advanced.

He loped along at the typical light trot of the Indians, expecting to arrive at the last settlement before nightfall. Just before coming near the settlement, when he could already hear the dogs barking, he had to wade across another river, somewhat narrower but rather deep in the middle, so that, feeling with his feet and his stick, he could sound his way through without swimming. That this river was the abode of a considerable herd of alligators was not known to him since nobody had told him. And since he knew nothing about the alligators infesting this river he waded fearlessly through. Quite obviously the alligators were entertained at the moment by something more important farther down or up the river and therefore paid no attention to Celso.

When Celso finally arrived at the settlement, he told the mayordomo in charge of the place: "This afternoon I got a fair impression of the jungle; an ugly, horrible trip."

The mayordomo crossed his legs, looked at Celso, rolled himself a cigarette into a maíze leaf and remarked casually: "This afternoon? Why certainly, you got yourself a fair idea of the jungle, quite so. Only the truth is that where you have been marching through, that's no jungle, that's our recreational park, where we take a walk on Sunday afternoons to stretch our legs. Two days march from here, there one meets a region where I usually say: now, this is where the world starts to be a bit closed in and not quite open to look through. But, my boy, don't get frightened. You see, generally tigers don't attack during the day, because that's when they take their nap. They are seriously interested in a good-looking boy like you only when you toss around in your sleep. But I know quite a lot of people who've never been bothered by a tiger. Of course I have to admit that all the others had no chance to tell their stories."

He licked his cigarette, lit it, and then went on. "I don't know anything of you, Chamula, but should you ever happen through here again, then perhaps you'll tell me how you got along with the tigers or how the tigers got along with you. And then if we have an opportunity to chat in a friendly way, I'll count you among the people who have not been bothered by tigers."

Recreational park for Sunday afternoons! It was now almost dark. Celso took a look around him. Barely thirty paces back of the mayordomo's primitive hut, the jungle lifted its steep wall of trees which covered the sky to such a height that if he wanted to look at the stars, he had to twist his head back at almost right angles to his neck. It was dark and tightly closed, inaccessible, apparently with no opening.

"What will you need for the road, Chamula?" asked the mayordomo. "I have some hard toasted tortillas, a special kind that will not become specky or moldy. You can't use any others. I also have rice, beans, raw sugar, freshly ground coffee and limes. I can also let you have fresh pozol. But only if you order it half a day in advance, so that it is fresh and won't get sour and moldy so quickly. And if you roll your own cigarettes I have sufficient fresh tobacco leaves, which are better and cheaper than wrapping paper, which I don't have anyway. Of course, I can let you have some cigarette paper. But I noticed that you smoke cigars and roll your own, so you don't need paper. Anyway, it will be better for you to spend tomorrow here and wait. We'll knead you some extra good pozol. You're in no hurry, are you? In this place it is like that; he who has to go through the jungle must not be in a hurry. It won't do him any good. Especially not if he finds himself in the middle of the grand selva insufficiently prepared. Take your time. The jungle won't run away, and the bridges won't be carried away, because there aren't any."

The mayordomo got to his feet and went into the hut, where he tried to get the smoke-soiled lantern to function properly. Night had closed in completely.

In the yard in front of the hut a sleepy fire was burning, spreading some light, enough to see as far as the picket fence around the yard.

Celso was sitting on a beam on the ground. The beam was the trunk of a tree with the bark partly peeled off. Nobody had taken pains to peel it off properly. In many places, the beam showed deep scars. These cuts had been made by people standing or sitting around with nothing else to do but play with their machetes.

"Take your time, you're in no hurry." This remark of the mayordomo came back to Celso now in the darkness of night. To him it sounded more like a warning and at the same time like a possible solution to his problems.

During the last two days he had been more and more influenced by the many stories he had heard and he had begun to look at his jungle march from an entirely different point of view. He had ceased to think of the two-peso reward for extra speed in delivering the letters. He busied his mind in searching for a solution by which his task might turn out less dangerous to him.

The instinct of self-preservation would not allow him to gamble recklessly with his life. He knew that he had only one life; and he felt it his duty not to risk this one life for papers and a few silver pesos reward.

He argued with himself thus: "I undertook to deliver the letters and the box, but if I perish in the jungle the letters will be lost, together with the box, and I can deliver to Don Eduardo neither the letters nor the medicines. Now, to be able to deliver the letters safely, I must protect my life. The surest way to protect it is not to march through the jungle alone but to wait instead for someone going the same way."

Consequently the strongest support of his reasoning was the mayordomo's remark: "Take your time, boy. Don't be in a hurry. Wait here."

When the mayordomo finally appeared with the smoking lantern, Celso was in a state of mind as calm as if he had to march only the well-known road from his native village to Jovel.

He scratched his bare feet, pulled out a thorn or two, examined his toes in search of niguas, those terrible sand fleas, tearing a dozen ticks, called garrapatas, out of his skin and rubbing the mosquito bites with a piece of camphor. All this he did with the philosophical calmness of the wandering Indian who won't have to march on the following day but is going to put in a rest day instead.

Once finished all these hygienic tasks, he took a jícara from his pack and asked the mayordomo where he could get some water.

The mayodomo was swinging lazily in a homemade hammock suspended from two beams of the porch, passing the time until supper was ready.

With a toe peeping out of his burst boot he pointed in a certain direction and said: "Right over there you'll find a brook— pure, clear, healthy and almost ice-cold water."

Celso disappeared into the darkness. He washed his hands, threw water in his face, drank out of his gourd, filled it again to the brim and went back to the long trunk where he settled down once more.

He withdrew a few paces from the porch, so as to put a greater distance between himself and the table set up on the porch, where the mayordomo would have his evening meal. Pulling his pack close to him Celso commenced to fumble in it.

Out of its depths he fished some rolled-up tortillas which were about to grow moldy. He produced some black-reddish dried meat that looked like fresh leather, then a fistful of black beans, cooked to the consistency of a mash and wrapped up in fresh banana leaves. That was followed by coarse-grain salt, carried in a dry corn leaf held together by a thin fiber string. A few green chile pods and a handful of green leaves were added to give his meal its accustomed taste.

He piled all that on a small mat of woven fiber, then stood up and stepped to the fire in the yard. The fire was always, day and night, at the disposal of the traveler, be he an Indian or a ladino, unless the host needed it temporarily for himself.

Celso pushed the embers around, put on some more wood,

and yard and hut immediately lit up. Against this sudden lighting, the black wall of the jungle looked all the more threatening.

Leaning the tortillas against the fire, Celso turned them, blew off the ashes and turned them over again. When they commenced to get crisp, he laid them upon hot embers pulled from the fire to keep them warm.

On a pointed stick he speared the dried meat and placed the stick on two forked branches driven into the ground. The beans he left in their banana leaf, but he placed the leaf also on the hot embers next to the tortillas.

The meat began to roast and he spread his entire meal on the little mat, which was placed near the fire. Now he turned the meat over a few times, took it off the stick and started eating.

Taking up a pinch of salt, he shoved it directly into his mouth. He ate his meat and the beans by tearing off a piece of tortilla, picking up the meat or the beans as though the piece of tortilla was a sort of little napkin, rapidly rolling the piece of tortilla into the form of a small cone and pushing this cone, filled with meat or beans, into his mouth.

Now and then he took a drink of water from the gourd which he had filled at the brook. He ate unbelievably slowly. Like all tired workers, he considered the meal part of his rest from hard work.

While he was still eating, an Indian maid began laying the table on the porch. Once the dishes, plates and tin cups had been set on the rough, shaky and unplaned mahogany table, the mayordomo's wife made her appearance. Fat and clumsy, she waddled like a duck. She was barefoot and on her body hung a long thin cotton skirt that touched the ground. It showed signs of considerable wear, as did the threadbare cotton blouse, half open at her breast.

As soon as the woman appeared on the porch, Celso got up from the fire, approached her, bowed and said: "Buenas noches, patrona." The woman replied lazily to his greeting with a short nod and, just to say something, asked: "Where you from, Chamula?" But when the youth answered she no longer listened, because it was a matter of complete indifference to her where the muchacho lived. She sat down on a very low, small stool. There were only two chairs. But the low stool seemed to appear more comfortable to the woman than any ordinary chair. And since she sat so low that her eyes just looked over the table, she took the plate into her lap.

When the woman started to eat, the mayordomo let out a loud and sonorous yawn, wriggled in his hammock, then got up, groaning as if, after a good long sleep, he had to undertake some disagreeable task.

Knives and forks were absent from the mayordomo's table. There were only a few spoons which, ages ago, might have looked like imitation silver, but which by now had been scraped and sanded so much that the leaden-looking tin was all that remained visible. The mayordomo's wife ate with her fingers, just as Celso did. She tore off a piece of hot tortilla, picking up the meat or the beans or the chile or the rice, doubled the little rag like a napkin over the food and shoved the whole package into her mouth.

The mayordomo would have loved to eat in the same way. But since he felt that, as a mayordomo, it was his duty to be different from all other mortals and command their respect, he used his pocket knife, picking up the food with it and lancing it into his wide-open mouth. Occasionally he used a spoon, but whenever he thought himself unobserved, and even his wife was not watching, he ate in exactly the same fashion as Celso.

The servant girls farther back, somewhere in the dark, were sitting on their haunches around a glowing fire on the ground. They could not be seen, but their talk and giggling could be heard. When they got too loud, the woman shouted at them:

"Damn you, you bitches, shut up or I'll club you on the head. Let's eat in peace."

For a while the girls would be scared and keep quiet. But after a short while they would start to giggle again until finally the woman took whatever she had at hand and threw it at them with a juicy oath.

When the girls started to take away the dented coffeepot, the mayordomo shouted: "Ven, Chamula, have some coffee."

Celso approached the table with his now empty gourd and the mayordomo poured the entire remains of the coffee into the gourd. "Gracias, patroncito," Celso said and went back to his fire, carefully balancing the gourd which was filled to the brim.

The coffee was black but it had been boiled together with brown crude sugar.

The woman got up from her stool. It demanded a tremendous effort on her part to rise to her feet. First she leaned over in front so that her nose practically touched her knees, then swung back rapidly, using this momentum to get up.

The mayordomo went back to his hammock and began to swing. He let his legs hang down on the sides of the hammock, his folded hands back of his head serving him as a cushion, and noisily sucked his teeth. Whenever he thought fit to help his digestion, he grunted and belched with satisfaction. Whether it was just out of pure well-being or out of a physical necessity, or just to tell his wife in this way that she was a good cook, was hard to tell. One might not be greatly mistaken if one assumed that he did so because he felt at home where he was the mighty sovereign who did not have to worry about pleasing anybody.

7

 In the meantime Celso, too, had finished his meal. He went to the brook with his jicarita, washed his hands, rinsed and gargled his mouth and, after filling the little vessel again with water, returned to the fire. Once he had collected his various objects and stowed them back in his net, he dragged the pack to the beam near the porch, pulled out one of the cigars he had rolled before, lit it with the aid of a glowing stick from the fire and, with the comfortable feeling of not having a care in the world, sat down on the trunk, leaning his back against a pole of the porch.

"Who sends you to Agua Azul?" asked the mayordomo, just to make conversation.

"Don Apolinar."

The mayordomo took some tobacco from his shirt pocket and rolled it into the white paper which was being sold as cigarette paper but which, in fact, was just ordinary newspaper.

Celso jumped to his feet with a glowing stick in his hand to light the cigarette for the mayordomo.

"It's a hell of a bad road to the montería. But at times it seems to me that it is easier to make it on foot than with saddle horses and pack mules."

As Celso did not say anything to that the mayordomo had no idea how to keep the conversation going. All the details which really mattered had been discussed.

But then he heard the sound of voices approaching. He cocked his ears, listened carefully and said: "Why! There they are now."

Celso, too, had heard the voices. When he looked in their direction he saw, emerging from the darkness, the figures of a man and a boy.

"Bueno, Don Policarpo, did you find your burros?" the mayordomo asked the man as soon as he came close.

"I did. All five were keeping together."

"They are all right?"

"In fine shape, gracias."

The man stepped onto the porch, and as he sat down on a chair which he pulled away from the table he saw Celso.

"Bueno, Chamula, como estás?" he addressed Celso.

Celso got to his feet, bowed and said: "Buenas noches, patrón."

"This here is Don Policarpo, a merchant from Socoltenango," explained the mayordomo. "He's been here already two days, getting his burros in shape for the trip. He also aims to march to the monterías. You might go along with him, Chamula."

There was nothing Celso had been hoping for more longingly during the past days than that someone, no matter who, would also have to go to the monterías.

However, he was no longer the awkward Indio he had been when he went to work at the coffee plantation. Since then he had changed thoroughly. And he knew it.

He had received his first lesson in how to get acquainted with the world he lived in when Don Sixto had deprived him of the money he had saved for his marriage. A second valuable lesson came when he could not buy a present for his mother because the storekeeper demanded three times the real price for the gift for no other reason than to sell him hard liquor instead. And another important change occurred in him when he learned from his father that Don Sixto had not been entitled to take the money away from him the way he did.

This bitter schooling he had received contributed to his newly acquired ability to think quicker and to say "yes" and "at your service, patroncito" slower. Since quick thinking and slow assenting had given him noticeable superiority in his dealings with Don Apolinar, he was resolved to apply this system in the future whenever he had a chance to do so. Before this change he would have said: "Patroncito, how lucky I am to have met you, because we can make the journey through the jungle together." But by now he knew that the immediate consequence of such frankness would be that the peddler would exploit him mercilessly to his own advantage.

He took a good look at Don Policarpo, watching him closely without seeming to do so.

Don Policarpo was of the same bronze color as was Celso. Short, thick-boned and sinewy, like Celso, he had the same black, slightly slanted eyes. And, like Celso, Don Policarpo had thick, black, wiry hair that grew so low on his brow and that gave the impression, as in the case of Celso, that he had a low, undeveloped brain, while the back part of his skull was dome-shaped and looked as if he were wearing a thick black turban or cap. There was no doubt that the two grandfathers, and possibly also the two grandmothers of Don Policarpo had been pure Indians in the service of townspeople, and that most likely the mother of Don Policarpo had married a mestizo and brought up her children in town. Thus Don Policarpo had become a ladino, standing on his own feet, independent because of his small ambulant commerce.

He spoke Spanish and Tsotsil as well as Tseltsal fluently. This, of course, was of great advantage in his trade, especially in respect to most other small merchants, who spoke only Spanish or Arabic. Since he not only spoke Indian, but looked Indian and, whenever he deemed it advantageous, assumed and applied Indian customs, he always won his customers' confidence in the small Indian villages and also that of the peons living on the large fincas. He was honest in his dealings, in his way, and content with less profit than any of the other small peddlers of Mexican or Arabian descent who roamed the country. The disadvantage lay in the fact that he possessed only a limited capital and therefore could travel with few goods.

None of this interested Celso. He did not know Don Policarpo's business problems. All he saw in Don Policarpo was a trader who made money. Although he recognized a fellow Indian in Don Policarpo, he paid him full respect as a ladino. And since Don Policarpo wanted to pass for a ladino, Celso considered him a link in the chain of those whom, somehow, he was going to use to get back the money which Don Sixto had taken away from him.

Celso gathered his courage. He took the risk of gambling with the offer to accompany the peddler.

"Perdóneme, patroncito," Celso said politely and humbly to the mayordomo, "excuse me, but I believe that I won't be able to travel with Don Policarpo."

"And why not, muchacho?" inquired Don Policarpo.

"You see," he addressed both men, "I've received orders from Don Apolinar to take the box of medicine to Agua Azul by the shortest route because the lumberjacks there are sick. They have malaria, paludismo, calentura, swamp fever, what do I know? Don Apolinar promised me two pesos extra if I get the box there as fast as possible."

Don Policarpo commenced to barter. "Don't worry about that, Chamula. Be reasonable. I know Don Apolinar well. He's my friend. I'll make it right with him. And I'm going to tell you something, muchacho, what's your name?—Celso? All right, Celso, I hope to transact some profitable business in the monterías. No traders have been there for months, I learned. I'm positive I'll sell everything I'm taking along. All right. Now, of course, you run on your legs much quicker than I, with my five donkeys; and I'll admit that you may lose that extra reward of two pesos if you travel along with me. But I'll make it good. I'll give you three pesos if you'll come along and we make the trip together."

The mayordomo said: "Listen, Chamula, you won't pick up three pesos that easily." Noisily he cleared his throat and spat into the darkness. Then he added: "And I told you already what a goddamned hell of a tough road it is. Not even the devil goes there to catch a soul. All souls remain in the jungle forever. But you'll see for yourself. Beyond La Culebra the real fun begins. You'd better take the three pesos and go along with Don Policarpo."

The mayordomo was highly desirous that everyone who came to the settlement with the intention of going to the monterías really went on his way. Because the sale of the provisions necessary to the travelers was one of his most important sources of income. Without that he probably would not have accepted the meager post of mayordomo, because the finquero who owned this forlorn cafetal, but who resided in Tabasco, only gave him a daily wage of two reales, twenty-five centavos. Of course he had chickens, raised hogs and had enough land to plant, with the help of the peons, but he needed profit from travelers.

Don Policarpo had no choice but to go to the monterías. He could not hesitate too long. Since for many months no trader had been in the monterías, one of the big ones might overtake him and satisfy the entire demand in those far regions. But in no case was he willing to make the trip by himself, with his little apprentice as sole companion.

Don Policarpo produced a package of cheap factory-made cigarettes, opened it and offered Celso a cigarette. Celso was still smoking his thick cigar. But he accepted the cigarette and tucked it into his shirt front.

"Now, don't be so stubborn, Celso," the trader said. "I want to go to the monterías with my junk. But you see, Chamula, I'm afraid, terribly afraid to march alone through that immense jungle. This boy here, who works for me, is a good, diligent boy. But he is still so little. On such a journey one needs somebody who can give a real hand when necessary. Now, look here, muchacho." Don Policarpo changed his tone and, almost pleading, he added: "I'll give you three pesos as far as Agua Azul if you come along with me. And I'll tell you something else: along the entire trip your food is on me. You won't have to spend one centavito. Of course, in exchange for your meals you'll lend me a hand once in a while along the road. In the mornings to search for the burritos and then in loading. Now be a good boy, Celso. You never know when we may meet again and I can do something for you."

"Bueno, patroncito," said Celso, "bueno, I'll go along with you. But I do it only because you haven't done much business lately. I certainly would not do it for anybody else. I would not cheat Don Apolinar. He's a good man and he trusts me."

"I told you already, Celso," replied the merchant, "I'll fix it with Don Apolinar so that he won't believe that you are delaying intentionally." He turned around to the mayordomo: "Don Manuel, couldn't your girls fix us some more coffee?"

"Why, of course, of course," said the mayordomo. Then he shouted: "Hey, Chucha, you goddamned loafer and lazy sow that you are, go and tell la patrona we want some more coffee. Hurry up if you don't want to be buried tomorrow, piojosas malditas, bunch of good-for-nothings in that kitchen!" With a terrific barking noise of his throat he spat again into the darkness.

Not on the following day, but one day later, the merchant, his apprentice, Celso with his pack on his back and the five donkeys carrying Don Policarpo's merchandise trekked along their way to the monterías.

The road was many times worse than the mayordomo had described it.

8

 It would have been the reverse order of the usual course of events had the heaviest work along the road not fallen upon Celso. He was willing and eager to earn the food which Don Policarpo had offered him. It had been agreed that for his maintenance he was to lend a hand here and there along the road. But because of Celso's willingness, on the second day of the march a commitment, if not an obligation, had already developed. Don Policarpo commenced to give definite orders as if he were the boss and Celso the servant.

It began when Don Policarpo, on arriving at the camping place the first evening of the march, let himself drop upon the ground, declaring to be so done in that he could not move a finger.

"Unload the burritos. I'll help you later," he said. And Celso, without help, unloaded the animals.

"Bring the packs over here," Don Policarpo ordered.

The little apprentice made every effort to appear before the eyes of Don Policarpo as if he were doing a lot of work. In fact, he only ran around, coiled up the pack ropes and put them away for the morning.

"We'll have to get some green stuff for the donkeys," said

Don Policarpo. But the "we" meant that Celso had to go with his machete, cut fresh leaves and carry them to the camp so that the donkeys might feed.

Don Policarpo fanned the fire to cook the food. But Celso had to fetch the water, get dry wood, wash the pots and see that the beans did not burn. In the morning, he had to gather the donkeys, put on the pack saddles, place the packs and rope and tie them properly. It is true that in this Don Policarpo lent him a hand and did what, according to the agreement, should have been Celso's part. When loading pack animals, one of two has to perform the heavy work. The easier part, such as handing over the lines and ropes for tying them firmly, falls to the other. In this case, Celso did the heavy work, the loading proper and the fastening and roping of the packs.

While Celso was searching for the burritos in the thicket, Don Policarpo enjoyed his breakfast. The donkeys, as soon as they had been packed, started on the way with Don Policarpo after them. Not until then did Celso have a few minutes to drink his coffee and warm himself a few tortillas. The coffee had been left by Don Policarpo in Celso's gourd, the tortillas were near the fire and the beans on one of the tortillas. So Celso ate. Once he had eaten he extinguished the fire with earth, took up his heavy pack and left at a double pace to overtake Don Policarpo. At last he reached the little caravan. He generally found that one of the animals, or even two or three, had knocked off their load against trees or rocks and he had to repack them. Or it might have happened that Don Policarpo had been careless and one of the animals had gone off into the thicket somewhere along the road. Celso, of course, had to search for the burro. And when he finally found it, it had either thrown its pack or the pack was dangling under the animal's belly. Celso could not load it by himself, so he freed the donkey from the pack, took it by the lead rope and carried the pack himself, dragging it as far as the spot where Don Policarpo was waiting with the other animals. And there he would repack the load with the help of the peddler.

Then again it would happen that the waiting animals would become impatient and Don Policarpo would be incapable of holding them back. So they would go on, with Don Policarpo after them, until the donkeys chose to stop somewhere and throw themselves on the ground. Celso, with the donkeys' packs on his back, had to run the entire stretch after Don Policarpo until he met him and, together, they would reload the packs. Then Celso had to retrace his steps on the run to fetch his own heavy pack, which he had left behind as he could not carry it on top of the others and pull the burro along at the same time.

But, here, in the jungle, the change in Celso's character continued. Once he became aware that Don Policarpo intended to exploit him to the last and realized that, while he might perhaps be tired, Don Policarpo was mainly lazy at Celso's expense, Celso underwent another change.

Climbing a very steep and rocky path, he slipped and fell with his pack, with such bad luck and right under Don Policarpo's eyes, that the trader could see how badly Celso had sprained his right arm. Celso, completely against his custom of hiding any signs of pain, groaned and showed a pain-racked face.

With his left arm he could not, as he claimed, cut green leaves off the trees. Therefore, the feeding of the donkeys was left to Don Policarpo. When loading the animals it was now Celso who passed the lines and the ropes under the donkey's belly to Don Policarpo, who was doing the loading. All along the march Celso got into the habit of trotting in the vanguard, driving one of the pack burros before him. He justified it by stating that the other donkeys followed more willingly which, by the way, was true. If one of the packs of the donkeys in charge of Don Policarpo slipped off, then Don Policarpo had to repack it with the help of his apprentice, and if the load on the donkey that Celso drove before him slid to one side, he waited until Don Policarpo came up.

This division of labor did not meet with Don Policarpo's approval. So one evening, after arriving in camp and unloading, he said: "Oye, Celso, you can very well use your left arm to cut the leaves of the trees. You are just as capable with your left as with your right arm."

"I'll try, patrón," said Celso. And that evening he produced a good load of fresh, green leaves.

Later in the evening, when they were squatting around the fire smoking, after supper, Celso said casually: "I don't think, patrón, that I can lose so much time on the road. The donkeys walk far too slowly and I've got to be in Agua Azul with my box of medicine in a hurry. Don Apolinar will surely beat me up if I don't get to Don Eduardo in due time with the medicine. All the people in the montería are sick."

In his few days of marching through the jungle Don Policarpo had obtained a sufficently impressive picture so as now to be scared out of his wits at the mere possibility that Celso would abandon the caravan, leaving him alone in the middle of the jungle. No matter whether he went on or returned, the simple thought of it made Don Policarpo sweat blood.

"Let's share a tin of sardines, muchacho," he said, pulling a pack toward him and searching inside until he produced a small tin of sardines in oil. These sardines constituted one of the few luxuries which Don Policarpo allowed himself when he had had a profitable day. At the same time, they constituted a sort of iron ration, an emergency food for cases when all other provisions had been destroyed by rain, rats or ants. His apprentice could not remember ever having seen him open one of those cans, although the merchant always carried at least six with him. A can of sardines was about the most expensive item of food the merchant could afford on his trips if one took into consideration his limited income.

The apprentice was given a sardine and a half, together with the privilege of licking the empty can. The remainder of the sardines and the oil were carefully divided into precisely two halves, one half for Don Policarpo and the other for Celso.

By this partition of the can of sardines, which was performed by Don Policarpo with as much ceremony and devotion as if he were performing the rite of Holy Communion, he accepted Celso as his equal and peer on the trip. He even went so far that, when anything was to be put on the fire or any other minor duty was to be performed, he called his apprentice to do it, telling Celso: "You just remain sitting on your hams, the chamaco can do that. He has nothing to do anyway. He doesn't even earn the salt he eats. You and I, we're both tired and the boy has young legs."

On the next day, marching through the jungle, when Celso shouted: "Patrón, patrón, el prieto is going to throw his load," Don Policarpo came running along, helped to push the load back into place and, when the little pack train was on the march again, he said: "Listen, Celso, simply call me 'señor.' That's shorter. If there's nothing to eat, you go just as hungry as I do."

After less than a day in the first montería which they reached, Don Policarpo had not a single spool of thread left for sale. All the wares which he had dragged along for weeks through fincas and little hamlets had been sold with excellent profit.

At ridiculously low prices he bought skins which he intended to take along so that the donkeys would not return empty and the return trip would pay. On those pelts he again would net a fair profit. He was only waiting for some company. Just as he had never had the intention of making the trip to the monterías alone, now he was even less inclined to return all by himself.

Celso still had to go two days farther than Don Policarpo,

who remained at the first montería. But Celso had no need to travel alone. Several men who were transferring to another camp on the opposite side of the river would take the same road.

Celso delivered the medicine box and the letters to Don Eduardo. He received his wages in cash because he explained that, for the moment, he was not thinking of returning and therefore a check would be useless to him. People who returned from the monterías, whether workers, employees, artisans or merchants, preferred to take along very little cash and the balance in checks, made out to the name of the bearer. Even the merchants who sold their wares here handed the cash over to the offices in the monterías in exchange for checks. Cash in coins weighed considerably, and every traveler, whether on foot or on horseback, limited the weight of his packs to the absolute minimum. The checks from the monterías were accepted everywhere like cash without any discount. At times, store owners in small towns of the state even paid a bonus of one or two per cent above the face value of the check. The transportation of cash from small villages to the larger towns and to the railway stations was too dangerous because of bandits roaming the country everywhere. No company insured cash remittances.

Celso had hoped to obtain work at Agua Azul. Yet Agua Azul, for the time being, was not taking on any labor. All the land acquired by this company for exploitation had been thoroughly worked over. The board of directors was at present dealing with the government to obtain new concessions for new lands. But such negotiations were apt to progress slowly. And before securing new concessions the montería would not hire workers. All the manpower required to float their enormous stocks of mahogany upon the arrival of the rainy season was on hand. Agua Azul, owned by Canadians and Scots, enjoyed among the workers the reputation of being the only montería where the worker was treated almost like a human being.

Celso had to be on his way again in search of another montería where he might hope to find work.

The monterías are not as close together as coal mines in Pennsylvania. Each montería has a territory the size of a European duchy, or of a medium-sized kingdom. Caoba trees don't grow close together, like pines. From the administrative building of one montería to the main administrative building of the next in any direction, a good two-day march was often necessary. Sometimes even three days were needed.

Celso did not have far to go. The next montería, which he reached after a day and a half, took him on. They would have taken on a drowned man if they had been certain that he could be revived at least well enough to do half a man's work. Agua Azul, even in full working season, had few labor requirements and paid better than any other montería. The worse the reputation of a montería, the lower the wages, and the more inhuman the treatment of the worker, the greater was the demand for replacements—not because the workers fled to look for work elsewhere, but because they were sacrificed unmercifully. Only their hands and arms were taken into account. Heads, souls and hearts were troublesome additions which had to be accepted into the bargain, but which would have been left out by the contratistas, had it been possible to do so. The peons' stomachs were also considered an unnecessary evil; but then men had to have stomachs just as steam boilers had to have fire boxes.

At one of these monterías Celso went to work. He might have walked on another day or two, attempting to find a better place. But soon he learned that, whatever place he might have found, it would have been worse than the one before.

The overseer or capataz, who at the same time was hangman, whip, slave-driver and torturer of the lumberjacks, felt Celso's hands, then the muscles of his arms, wrists and legs. "Have you already worked with the ax?" he asked.

"Not much with the ax, but I'm a good machetero," replied Celso. "I worked in coffee fincas for several years, mostly with the machete."

"Four reales per day," said the capataz, "and ten pesos for myself, because I take you on. The ten pesos will be deducted from your first pay. If you run away it's one hundred and fifty lashes for the first time and fifty pesos fine. You probably won't attempt it the second time, because then you'll get your whipping and on top of it be hanged. Ask your fellow jacks what's meant by that. You buy only at the tienda of this montería. And from an itinerant peddler you buy only with permission from the manager. So now you've been taken on. One year irrevocable contract. You were lucky to save yourself the tax on the contract. But with or without contract-tax, don't think you can wander off when you feel like it. One year's the minimum. We don't hire for less than a year. Name?—Age?—Village?—Bueno, all right. You belong to contractor Don Gregorio's gang."

From the fifty centavos which Celso was getting per day, twenty centavos were deducted and paid to the cook of the gang for food. Occasionally Celso felt like smoking and so he had to buy tobacco leaves. He needed camphor to heal mosquito bites as well as the bites and stings of other insects and of reptiles. Now and then quinine was distributed in doses by the management when heavy attacks of fever became too frequent —and when there was any quinine available at all.

Occasionally he had to buy tallow to be used as ointment for his back after a whipping. Whippings were given not only for flight, which anyway was very rare, but for many other infringements of the manifold rules in existence and of which one was the most frequent: insufficient daily production or timber carelessly trimmed. No consideration was given to the possible causes of lack of production. There were many causes of which the man was absolutely innocent, such as bad axes or half-broken pulling hooks, and natural obstacles presented by the jungle and by meteorological conditions. Neither fever nor any other sickness or disease was an excuse for the failure to deliver the prescribed daily quota of two tons of sound, properly dressed trunks, called trozas, ready to be pulled out. At certain places in the jungle only young trees of no value were found, or old, deteriorated, worm-eaten trunks; and there would be still others where the Indian had to cut his path with the machete to find adequate trees. This sometimes took hours. But it was not put down in favor of the jack. Every day he had to deliver two tons, fourteen tons a week, of first-class caoba ready to be hauled to the river. How he achieved it was his affair. He was paid for the delivery of the timber.

When he managed, owing to specially favorable circumstances, to produce three or even four tons on a single day, he was credited the excess production occasionally, according to the whim of the contractor or the foreman of his gang, in compensation for a meager day within the same week. Yet when this meager day fell into the next week he lost his credit. In the majority of the cases, or one might say always, the contractor forgot the excess tonnage of a favorable day and only put down the deficit of the lean days and noted down the man's name for the so-called "fiesta."

Celso spent less for clothes than ten per cent of what an American spinster spends on the clothing of her lap dog. He worked naked and thus did not need shirts or pants. A cheap cotton rag around his hips as a loincloth constituted his entire working outfit. Since there were no Sundays or holidays and work went on each and every day from sunrise to sundown, the men did not need anything to dress for a holiday. If, in beneficial circumstances, they had produced their daily task of two tons, they were free to celebrate the rest of the day. Supposing that they managed to gain such a quarter rest day, which happened rarely enough, they went to bathe in the river, picked the niguas and their eggs from between their toes, healed cuts, sores and wounds in their skin, cut out thorns and splinters from their bodies or from under their fingernails or fried themselves a tasty iguana or a tepescuintle, if they had been lucky enough to catch one, thus forgetting at least once in a while the monotonous taste of the eternal sun-dried meat, rice and black beans boiled in water and condimented with green or red chile.

As the owners of the monterías were stout patriots, or at least pretended to be, the only rest day during the year was the sixteenth of September, which was celebrated in commemoration of the Declaration of Independence of the country from the Spanish Crown. The Republic had given its citizens unlimited liberty for making money, something which the monarchy of Spain had never done. In consequence, this revolutionary holiday was, for them, as sacred as the prophet's beard is to a Mohammedan. The company even paid this day as if it were a working day, and with this generous attitude the owners meant to display their patriotic feelings. The only problem with these opulent republican shows was the fact that in the gangs, working in the depths of the jungle, and having contact with the administrative building only once in every two or three months, no calendar could be found. In the majority of the cases, even the contratista, the production chief of the gang, did not know whether it was Sunday, Wednesday or Friday. He had a very hazy idea that it must be October or December. In his little book he only put down so many working days and so many tons every day. When, for some reason, it became absolutely necessary to establish the exact date of a given day, he counted back to the day of the departure of the gang from the front yard of the administration building. That day at least was fixed, because it was the day on which the contract had started. By counting back the days he was able to establish the date of today more or less accurately. But all this counting back and forth tired him, so finally he gave up and left it to the President of the United States and to the Prime Minister of Great Britain to find out from their calendars what day it was.

At any rate, the contractor of a gang had no need to know the date. Although his contract ran for a certain term, two years, three or five, he was not paid by the day or by the month but according to the tonnage of caoba delivered at the main floating station of the river which served for final transportation to the seaport.

And since nobody in the gang knew with certainty whether the sixteenth of September, the birthday of the Republic, was today or tomorrow or sometime within the next two weeks, work went on that day just as on any other working day. As the men were working anyway, they were paid for this day. Thus the owners loyally completed their legal duty of compensating the workers for the Independence Day. In the administration building the day was of course duly and highly celebrated. Because there, to the wall, was nailed a calendar. And everyone from the general manager down to the lowest paid office worker got blind drunk to prove how solemnly he regarded celebration of that national holiday.

9

 Celso thought only of his marriage and of his fifteen children whom he intended to bring into this world with the help of his girl. This constant thought made him support all the misery of his present life. With every new evening when he dropped on his mat dead tired, the amount which he had set out to obtain grew. Since he did not think of anything but earning that sum, to prove to the girl's father that he was willing and capable of being a good and faithful provider and spouse to the girl, he bought very little at the montería tienda, except absolutely unavoidable necessities. After a certain time he needed a new mat. He bought himself a good pocket knife, because his old one was worn out and the blade had finally broken. He needed a heavy blanket for the cold nights during the rainy season. His mosquito net began to rot and presently fell to pieces. He had to buy a new one, because out there even an Indian cannot sleep without a mosquito bar. Some time ago he had paid off the ten pesos to the capataz for hiring him.

After he had passed a full year in the montería and had counted the cash to his credit at the administration, adding what he had earned for the delivery of the letter and for his help to

Don Policarpo, he found that all his earthly possessions amounted to exactly fifty-three pesos and forty-six centavos.

However, this money was not enough to make the impression that he had in mind on the girl's father. He wanted to own no less than eighty pesos in heavy silver when he left the montería.

To earn that amount of money he had to hire himself out for a second year. Since he remained in the same gang and had astutely managed to be offered the job for an additional year by the same contratista, he saved the ten pesos commission which some leech would have collected.

The second year seemed to pass quicker for him than the first. He had developed into one of the best ax-men and trimmers. He also had learned to select his trees with great skill and to choose carefully the best side of the tree to cut and how high to build the platform on which he stood to fell the tree. On many days he would finish his daily quota early in the afternoon. Frequently he helped some poor beggar of a newcomer, who was unable to discharge his task and who therefore ran the risk of being put down in the book for the "fiesta." After the first half of the second year, the contratista paid him five reales per day, instead of the four agreed upon. Of course the contratista did not do this out of the kindness of his noble Christian heart, but to win Celso perhaps for a third year. Celso had been wise enough not to tell anyone that he was working only to earn a certain amount and that he would leave once he had enough money. Even on the final day he did not admit that he was leaving for good, but said that he was going to see his father and mother and would be back after a few weeks. From his fellow workers' experience he had learned to watch out for himself and take care not to walk into one of the many traps set to get retiring workers back on the hook.

To hook workers again who had finished their contract was the business of human parasites, the so-called coyotes, who infested the monterías and their recruiting districts. They were scavengers, feeding on carrion left over by the big labor agents who hooked their men in the far interior of the state.

It was comparatively easy work to catch men again who had finished their contracts, to catch them through fraud, tricks, alcohol or with the aid of harlots from the lowest strata, whores so low that the only place where they could hope to do business was a montería. Very few men, and only those of very strong character and will power, escaped these coyotes.

When contracts expired the coyotes went hunting. They gathered in groups and searched villages, hamlets, settlements and fincas near the jungle for escaped criminals who occasionally hid there. The authorities offered no reward for catching criminals. But the coyotes paid from five to ten pesos to those who revealed the hiding places of convicts or fugitives from justice. Small rancheros living in constant fear of escaped criminals who assaulted them and threatened their lives did their best to rid themselves of this plague.

The coyotes were not a bit concerned about the moral past of their catches; they were only interested in a pair of strong arms. When on the hunt they assumed an air of authority and frequently, when the fugitives were armed, had to fight serious battles to catch them. The captives were tied up so well and guarded so closely that it would have been easier for them to escape from a well-built prison than from these manhunters. Manacled, in file, they were dragged through the jungle. The least infringement on any order during the march got them such a lashing that they barely had a shred of skin left whole when they arrived at the monterías.

Any idea of escape was given up after the failure of the first attempt, because the penalty for attempted escape was hanging. These hangings were all the more terrifying and destructive of any resistance because they were not deadly. Had they caused death they would have been less impressive. The coyotes never hanged anyone with the intention of killing them. A dead man would not have brought them any money. Only the live brought returns.

The enganchadores, that is, the regular labor agents, bought Indians from prisons in the villages by paying the fine for the Indian to the mayor of the village or to the secretary of the Government who acted in the village on behalf of the State Government as registrar, statistician, postmaster and telegraph operator. The fines imposed upon the Indian population were considered one of the main sources of a secretary's income. Against the fine paid the prisoner was delivered to the concessioned agents, and the agents sold the prisoners to the monterías. At the montería, before he was credited any wages, the Indian thus sold had to work off the fine paid for him by the agent, in addition to the high recruiting commission for the agent and the state tax on the contract.

Naturally the coyotes attempted to hook workers as cheaply as possible to increase their profits. They never bought Indians from prisons. Such an expenditure would have been money thrown out the window. They made night raids into small villages, broke open the jails and kidnaped the prisoners. In the morning, when the secretary saw the doors broken open he believed, like the rest of the village, that the prisoners themselves had broken jail or that they had been liberated by their friends. Nobody, not even their own families, expected the escaped prisoners to return voluntarily, because upon their return they were subject to increased sentences or fines. So they simply disappeared. The coyotes, to put the fear of God into the prisoners, told them that, unless they came along voluntarily to the monterías, they would be denounced to the judge for breaking jail and for asking the coyotes to take them to the monterías. The coyotes convinced the Indians that a jail break and the destruction of the doors or the walls, even though they were built only of adobe, would be considered destruction of a public building and be punished by death. The Indians knew perfectly well that the judge would believe the coyote who was a ladino, and that everything had happened exactly as told by the ladino. A ladino always spoke the truth whereas an Indian always lied.

Every jack in the monterías whose contract was about to expire lived in constant fear of the coyotes. Workers knew from tales and evidence that there was no misdeed, no crime, that a coyote would hesitate to commit if he could land a man again on his hook. No worker was safe from the guiles of these racketeers except the one who was dead and buried.

For all these reasons Celso did not tell anybody that he intended to leave the monterías for good. The changed behavior of the boss of his gang was another reason for his discretion in the matter. He had noticed that his boss, the contratista, never mistreated him and assigned him to good locations and fine trees. He saw in Celso an extra good worker of whom he wanted to be sure for another two years.

Almost from the beginning of his second hitch Celso started to mention in conversations that he would have to go home for some four weeks to see his parents and bring them the money earned to buy some cattle. Astutely he wove into the conversation the fact that he had to work another two years at the montería to accumulate sufficient money so that his father could purchase a certain piece of land on which he, Celso, would settle when he returned after another two years, and marry and live peacefully in his village.

10

 The day when Celso had terminated his second year at the montería finally arrived. But if he left at once he would have to march through the jungle all by himself. Therefore he waited a few days until a large group of released men would leave for La Feria de la Candelaria in Hucutsin.

The Candelaria fair in Hucutsin represented for the caoba workers something like the rewards of a large port of call in South America for sailors after a long, hard trip across a storm-beaten ocean.

The vast majority of the montería workers' contracts began with the Candelaria fair in Hucutsin. Here they came to know and, if willing to spend the money, to enjoy all those earthly delights which, in the small world from which these men hailed, were considered the greatest and the most sinful pleasures imaginable. If considered soberly by anyone who happened to arrive during the height of the festivities and who had seen similar saints' feasts in other towns of the Republic, this fair really appeared rather meager, emaciated, dull and dry. But hundreds of Indian peasants and farm workers saw such a carnival for the first time in their lives. From the limits of their small villages and their monotonous existence this festivity assumed in their eyes the aspect of the biggest, most beautiful, gayest, most voluptuous and luxurious celebration that could be imagined.

Consequently, the deeper the contract workers penetrated the jungle the more brilliant and intoxicating the Candelaria fair became in their memory. Whatever fancies they might entertain during the days or nights in the jungle, whatever extravagant thoughts and earthly desires might arise within them, were always linked to the Candelaria fair: to buy a bright-colored serape or blanket, to get thoroughly drunk or to gamble, or to watch the dances and performers in the carpas, the tents put by itinerant comedians, or to hold a passionate girl in their arms, even if she was a professional, or to inhale the smoke of the candles and the incense in the church, or to have a fight with another boy, or to see the women and girls bartering at the counters, to listen to the brass music of bare-footed Indian musicians in the streets and to stand there for hours doing nothing but enjoying the enchanting melancholic ballads of the corrido singers or, well—there were a hundred other wonderful things to behold and to do. Throughout the long months of merciless hard work in the jungle so many vari-ous wishes arose in their minds that eternity would not suffice to satisfy them all.

The nearer the days of the Candelaria fair approached, the more excited the lumberjacks became. And just as seamen in port, after long weeks on the high seas, behave in bars, brothels and on dance floors, so the caoba workers acted when they arrived at the Candelaria fair after long years imprisoned in the jungle. And exactly as sailors, who during their voyage were firmly resolved to marry, settle down and raise chickens, spend their entire earnings in three days and three nights in taverns, dance halls and bordellos and then have to sign on again for a new long trip because they have not even enough money left to buy a bus ticket from New York to Harrisburg, so dozens of workers homeward bound from the monterías, after half a week's celebration are seen running after an enganchador, asking him to be kind enough to hire them again. The enganchador, hunting the taverns during the festivities like a hungry lizard after a sugar-fattened fly, willingly gives the man a fifty-peso advance on the new labor contract.

And of course the man immediately converts these fifty pesos into the purchase of more pleasure. One week after having returned from the monterías, he wakes up, finds that he's an ass and, after another week back in the jungle again, begins to dream of the delights and the enchantment to be enjoyed at the Candelaria fair two years hence.

Celso was not to be caught that easily. The Candelaria fair with its various pleasures did not appear to him as the promised paradise in which all desires come true. No enganchador, not even the smartest coyote, could have used the fair as a bait to get him on his hook.

It had certainly been a very bright idea of the first labor agents who engaged men for the monterías to consider the Candelaria fair the beginning and the end of a labor contract. However, Celso was no inexperienced Indian yokel who knew nothing about the world and its snares. He had seen similar festivities in the small towns of the Soconusco district where he had worked on coffee plantations. Often he had attended the important San Juan fair at Chamula. He had visited fairs in Jovel and Balun Canan. To him the Candelaria fair was not sufficiently exciting to dull his senses and make him forget what it meant to work in a montería for two long years or to make him lose sight for an instant of why he had gone to slave in the jungle in the first place.

While the majority of the men still in the jungle dreamed of how they would make up for the miseries and sufferings of a year or of several years during the fair, Celso dreamed of nothing but marriage and fifteen children. Compared to the good things he wanted, all the glamour of the saint's feast seemed to him like an inflated, bright-colored rubber balloon which is good to look at for a while, but shrinks in the evening and is swept away with the rest of the garbage.

11

 Days before, Celso's gang boss had intimated to the manager of the montería that Celso very likely might not return. The montería could not afford to lose a powerful, highly skilled cutter like Celso. So the manager sent a letter with another boy marching in the same group to Don Gabriel, the agent who would be in Hucutsin for the fair to deliver an important troop of new men.

The letter contained several instructions concerning the recruitment of workers. The instructions referring to Celso read as follows: "One more thing, Don Gabriel; a certain Celso, a Chamula youth from Ishtacolcot, has drawn all his wages and I suspect he intends not to get on the hook again. We cannot do without him. He is too good an ax-man to be lost. I shall give you an additional fifty pesos for this boy, apart of course from the usual commission. This muchacho is passing through Hucutsin with the group of retiring men and it will be easy for you to locate him there."

For an extra fifty pesos Don Gabriel would have dug up a corpse, revived him and hired him for the montería. To catch a live worker was a cinch, and it was many times simpler if he happened to be an Indian. Whether this Indian intended to visit his dying mother or thought of marrying or wanted to save his old father from losing his little farm was no concern of Don Gabriel. Don Gabriel had to support a wife, his mother and his mother-in-law. Therefore he could not reflect upon the feelings of others, much less on those of an Indian who was not even sufficiently civilized to have the feelings of a proper human being. An Indio! Bah! An animal that can speak and laugh but is still just an animal!

On the very day on which the letter from the montería arrived in Hucutsin, the pushers working for Don Gabriel had discovered Celso in the troop of workers who had come from the monterías to visit the fair. From that moment on they did not lose sight of him for an instant.

Watching his every move, they were disappointed to find Celso did not drink. To get the victim drunk and catch him in his drunkenness was the easiest and, therefore, the most common trick. Celso was not averse to a glass of strong comiteco once in a while, but he would never drink when he realized it might somehow get him into trouble. His two years in the montería had given him enough second-hand experience from his comrades about the working system of the enganchadores and the coyotes.

Soon he had become aware that there were always two mugs near him no matter where he went, and that they were always the same two mestizos, dressed in cheap small-town fashion. They were the type from which the monterías selected their overseers, the so-called capataces or cabos. During the recruiting of contract labor they were used as pushers, or game-drivers; they were those who, on behalf of the agent or the coyote, carried out the snatchings, the fights, the knifings and any other sordid acts indirectly suggested by the agent. The agent kept his hands clean in the eyes of the law and, when things became too hot, the drivers disappeared temporarily. They were supported by the agent and returned when the odor of the crimes committed had blown off or when friends of the agent came into public office.

The agent was a respectable ladino, a real caballero who practiced the recruiting of caoba workers as an honorable trade. He was properly licensed and therefore protected by law. The shabbiness of the trade fell to the pushers, who were not interested in pretending to be decent and honest citizens. They were far more sure of their income doing the dirty work for an agent than if they had been on their own as bandits or footpads. Being the tools of an agent, they enjoyed a certain protection, just as hoodlums do in the pay of racketeers who in turn are backed by influential politicians.

As soon as Celso saw the two characters circling around him he guessed the contents of the letter which he was certain had been sent to the agent. He realized that from now on anything could happen. There was only one crime of which he need not be afraid: murder. He would not be murdered, because nobody was interested in a dead Indian, not even the devil who, as every Indian knew, selected exclusively white people, ladinos, that is, to broil in hell.

Celso was afraid. His was the fear of a man who knows the trap is set for him but who, at the same time, sees that he is unable to avoid running into it, whatever he may attempt to do.

He began to ponder over various plans for fooling the drivers. First he thought of sending the money to the girl's father and then escaping while on the march to the monterías. But the more he considered this plan the more useless it appeared. There was nobody in Hucutsin whom he could trust with the money. Nobody was there from Ishtacolcot or from any of the neighboring villages. And he could not think of sending the money by mail. In that case, he would have to hand over his hard-earned money to a post official, another ladino.

Of course nobody could drag him by force to the monterías. There had to be a contract. Once a contract existed it would not help him much to be successful in his flight. The authorities were paid twenty-five pesos tax for legalizing the contract so that in the case of escape the police would catch and return the runaway.

For some time Celso thought of paying his shadows five pesos, so that they would leave him alone. But his fellow workers' experiences had taught him that even if he paid the pushers they would still continue to work for the agent, who would also pay them five pesos, and thus they would make ten pesos. Whatever Celso might offer them, they would take his money and still betray him since, in every case, besides the money received from Celso, they would get five pesos on top of it from the agent. Even if the agent paid them only two pesos for their job, they would still betray Celso, because it meant two pesos on top of what they got from Celso. No matter what Celso paid them, they would sell him anyway, for the agent was a permanent customer and Celso was not. They were loyal to their agent. Sometimes even the lowest scum is loyal and sticks to his word, even if only temporarily and under certain conditions.

Celso had thought of remaining three days in Hucutsin. In the first place he wanted to rest and heal the wounds he had received on his march through the jungle. And also he wanted to listen to the corrido singers and to the itinerant musicians; go to church and offer a candle to the Virgin for his safe return from the monterías; buy some presents for his mother, for his girl, for the girl's father and for his own father.

Throughout the two years' absence from home, he had not been able to send any message to his parents, and in turn he himself had received no word from them, for none of the family could read or write. The beginning and the end of his formal education had consisted in his mother's teaching him to cross himself correctly, to sprinkle himself with holy water when entering church, to kneel decently before the various images and to say a brief Ave Maria. Why all this had to be done he did not know and his mother had not been able to explain it to him because she, herself, had learned it in turn from her mother without any explanation. Even had he had the best of intentions to send a brief note back home, nobody could have helped him, as none of his fellow workers knew how to write. And none, himself not excepted, had the necessary leisure to compose a letter. During the long months in the jungle, working ceaselessly, all their interests in life fell to such a level that only by their human aspect were they distinguishable from the oxen and the mules that worked side by side with them. All their requirements were limited to sleeping, eating and delivering a minimum of two metric tons of trimmed caoba a day. They had no other desire than that of finding good trees, easy to fell, and no other thought than that of escaping a whipping, or worse, being hanged at night. To write letters was as far from their minds as was the idea, for an ox, to explore the South Pole.

When Celso noticed the two men stalking him, he gave up his plan to spend a few days in Hucutsin. He decided to elude them by a few deft turns and twists in the festive crowd, and to march off late at night and reach the high pass of Teultepec. The path over this high pass was far more difficult than the road passing through Sibacja. Consequently the hirelings would assume that he was going to choose the easier and shorter route via Sibacja. He was certain they would follow him on the easier road as soon as they discovered he had outsmarted them.

Taking into consideration all the possibilities that might confront him, an unexpected departure in the middle of the night seemed the only way open to Celso to deceive his shadows. If he remained in Hucutsin even for one more day, he might lose against their cunning. They could not waste too much time on just one snatch. Many other men were marked already by the agents to be hooked. The three or, at best, five pesos which they received for Celso would not fatten them. They had to work fast on Celso to be ready for other prey. Celso, by sheer instinct, knew that his chance was now or never.

Had he not been bothered with his pack, it would have been easier for him to escape unnoticed. Baggage is always an obstacle to speedy travel. However, his pack contained all his earthly possessions, except for the money he had received on presenting his check in town, which he now carried wrapped up in his woolen sash.

Camping close to the adobe wall of a house under the widely protruding shingled roof, he had several other youths of his tribe for companions. When one of them went for a walk there was always another one on guard, watching the packs.

The two men who were after Celso watched his pack more closely than his person. They knew full well that an Indian on the road cannot abandon his pack because the pack contains everything he needs on his long marches: his petate, on which he sleeps, his woolen blanket, mosquito bar, pitch-pine splinters to build a fire, huaraches for thorny or sharp-stoned stretches and for those parts of the trail which are covered with sharp-edged clam-shells, deposited there in unknown, remote geological ages, perhaps hundreds of millions of year ago. Since in those regions ordinary matches are as good as useless, he carries a piece of steel, flint and matchwick in his pack. He also carries raw tobacco leaves and sun-dried meat, mashed cooked beans, tortillas, salt and green vegetable leaves needed to season his food and provide important vitamins for his diet. Without his pack and without his machete, an Indian on the march is almost helpless.

It was his pack that had made Celso realize that coyotes were after him. Shortly after arriving in town he opened it to take out some tobacco leaves, and happened to notice that the two were talking to one another rapidly, pointing to the pack as if to memorize its peculiarities. For a few moments Celso thought they intended to rob him. But immediately it occurred to him that mestizos had no use for the pack of an Indian; they would not be able to sell anyone its contents or even part of them. However important the pack might be for its owner, an Indian, it is valueless for anyone not an Indian. Celso knew that his pack was of no intrinsic value and that nobody would give him two reales for it, except another Indian.

Now he began to consider possible ways of taking away his pack without the two drivers noticing it. He thought of arranging with other Indian boys to take the pack somewhere to the outskirts of the town where he would pick it up and be on his way. Or of leaving the pack in some little store and fetching it on the following day. He himself would spend the night outside the town under a tree. This way he might mislead the snatchers and make them believe he had already escaped.

But everything he thought of, his persecutors seemed to have considered. He had to invent something absolutely new and completely unexpected to escape unnoticed.

As soon as these hounds finished their tasks in town, once the saint's feast was over and the march to the monterías started, they would get jobs as drivers. Not as drivers of pack animals, but as drivers of Indians contracted for the caoba camps. It was up to them to keep the troop together, to see that nobody straggled behind, tried to break ranks or attempted to run away. For this purpose, they were given whips, lassos and good horses, yet no agent would ever trust them with a gun.

These hirelings were crazy for a chance to shoot an Indian, to enjoy the sadistic pleasure of watching the painful dying of a mortally wounded human being. They would invent any sort of accusation to justify to the agent that they had had no other recourse but that of killing the runaway or the slacker. And they killed when quite certain that the agent could not successfully investigate a reported mutiny.

Had they been trusted with guns, the agent might have delivered barely one-half of the men recruited to the monterías, because the other half would have been shot along the march for mutiny or for an attempted attack on the drivers. The agent had to be constantly on the lookout to prevent the drivers from hanging a man who remained in the rear, just to amuse themselves. He had sufficient other means of punishing mutinous workers along the march, and punishing them so that they would have preferred death by shooting. To deliver men alive and capable for work was the agent's main object. The monterías did not pay for men shot on the road.

Once the workers had been delivered, complete in number, the most brutal of the drivers remained as capataces with the groups they had driven through the jungle.

It was not just a matter of the few pesos which the drivers got for each man enlisted, it was the prospect of an agreeable job as capataces which moved them to serve their masters with devotion. Against the sadistic inclinations of the drivers, Celso had no weapon which might protect him. As matters stood, suicide would be the only sure way out. Murdering the two bloodhounds would not liberate him. Within one hour he would be sentenced to pay five thousand pesos, which he would have to earn in a montería. Thus the drivers would actually have been murdered in favor of an agent's commission.

Had Celso been able to guess the drivers' plan, even then he would have had no chance of escape. The way the two mestizos had planned to get him within the next few hours was so clever that only a miracle could have saved him.

12

Celso began getting ready for his trip home. His idea was to steal away during the night. He hoped the two hounds would get drunk, or go to sleep, or bed a whore. Lowdown as they were and tough as they pretended to be, they were human beings, subject to human needs. They had to sleep sometime.

It was around eleven at night. Although the town was the commercial center of a district of some thirty thousand square miles, it had no street lighting. The politicians in power preferred to spend public funds on feasts, fireworks, banquets, receptions, street decorations and monuments of heroes and presidents rather than street lighting, a water supply and drainage, which would not have given them a personal advantage.

Nevertheless, during the Candelaria fair enough light at night came from candles stuck into bottles and lanterns hung in windows and from the merchants' oil and kerosene lamps which were dimly lighting the streets. Some merchants left their lamps burning throughout the night to avoid thefts of their merchandise, which was covered with tarpaulins on counters and in booths. Any town in the Republic where a saint's festive day was celebrated was as full of merchants as of thieves, robbers, pickpockets, counterfeiters, whores, pimps, gamblers and con men.

Cautiously Celso got up and slipped along the street to investigate. He did not see the two mestizos, or any other man who gave the impression that he might be in cahoots with them.

Thus, finding the coast clear, he went back to the porch where he had meant to spend the night and silently lifted his pack. One of the boys resting on the same brick floor woke up while Celso took his pack.

The youngster lifted his head and asked: "What is it? Going away?"

"No," replied Celso. "I'm only going to look for another place to sleep. It's too cold here and besides it's too full of fleas."

Satisfied with the reply, the youngster stretched, grunted and immediately fell asleep again.

Celso was afraid the boy might have talked too loud and that one of the hunters might have heard talk about moving away. So he remained on his haunches for a long while. When he heard no noise other than that which came from the stalls of the merchants, he felt reasonably safe.

With far greater silence and caution than the first time, he again lifted his pack and eased toward the deep shadow in the corner of two adjacent adobe houses. Here, in the darkness, he adjusted the straps of the supporting front band and finally arranged the pack on his back. He was ready to leave.

Bending as deeply as the pack would allow, always keeping in the shadow of houses, he hurried down the street. At the end of the street he turned left to gain a path which went along the outskirts of the town. He intended to follow this path until he came close to the old cemetery. There he would turn left again and, after some more twists and crossings, would reach the mule path which led to the high pass of Teultepec.

When he had left the last house at the northwest corner of

the town and was just about to turn toward the old cemetery, three men jumped up in front of him.

"Hey you, Chamula," one of them shouted, "where are you goin' in the middle of the night with that stolen pack?"

"Nothing stolen," Celso said, stopping. "This is my pack, and I got to be on my way early if I want to make Oshchuc this afternoon."

"Where are you from, Chamula?" asked the second man.

"No damn business of yours."

"You getting fresh, son?" said the third, pounding his fist into Celso's ribs.

"Well, what do you want from me?" asked Celso, although he knew only too well what they wanted, because, even in the dark, he had been able to recognize his two persecutors.

"We've got the same right to be on the road at night as you, or don't you think so?" said one of them.

"Of course you have," replied Celso, "and now I'm on my way."

He turned around to go on. But one of them hit him a strong blow against the head. Celso stumbled and was thrown off balance by his heavy pack. Another man landed on top of him. Celso wanted to free himself, and exchanged blows with the one who had fallen on him.

When the two men saw Celso on the ground, fighting to free himself, they ran a few steps toward the houses, shouting wildly: "Policía, policía, policía, asesinos, murderers, auxilio, help!"

Fifteen seconds later, two policemen appeared on the scene.

Celso jumped up and tried to run away without his pack. But the man with whom he had been fighting on the ground was prepared for that. He tackled Celso around the legs so that he stumbled again. When he finally freed himself with a blow of his fist and was about to run, the policemen threw their clubs between his legs. One of the hounds jumped on the stumbling

Celso, threw him down and held him on the ground until the policemen took Celso firmly by the arms and pushed their shotguns into his back. The man who had been fighting with Celso on the ground now yelled at the top of his voice: "He tried to kill me, the stinking Chamula. He cut me in the leg with his knife, right here. What a misfortune. Now I'll lose my leg. Look here, sargentos, right here I got the knife with which this Chamula swine intended to kill me and ripped open my leg. There's the knife."

Celso knew that his knife was in the pack, wrapped up in a rag, together with the dried meat.

Then one of the policemen told him: "Bueno, bueno, Chamula, pick up your pack. We will see the jefe and hear what he has to say about this case."

There was no escape for Celso. With his heavy pack on his back, it was impossible for him to run, and the slightest attempt to throw off the pack would only have caused the policemen, who were following him closely, to club him over the head. But even if he had been able to escape the police, who perhaps had no special interest in arresting him, he would not have been able to escape the two drivers. Every time they passed some dark corner where flight would have been possible and where, owing to the darkness, the police would not have been able to use their old-fashioned firearms successfully, those two stayed so close to his side that he could only take very short steps.

He was brought to the office of the chief of police. The jefe sat there in his shirt sleeves, with half a week's stubble on his face, thoroughly drunk.

"What's the matter with that Chamula?" he asked the policemen.

"Street brawl with these people."

"I did not fight, mi querido jefecito," said Celso shyly. He still had his pack on his back.

"Testigos, witnesses?" asked the chief.

"Yes, three, here they are," said one of the policemen, pointing to the three men.

"And he knifed me in the leg, right here," said one of them loudly and hastily.

"Knifed you in the leg? With that knife? Where?" asked the chief.

The man rolled up his trouser leg, and there really was blood on his cotton trousers. He even showed the knife wound. But he did not come too close to the desk of the drunken chief, who was barely able to open his eyes. What little he was capable of seeing became even more hazy because his office was lighted only by a smoke-covered lantern and a candle which had been stuck on his desk with its own droppings. No doctor examined the wound for the simple reason that there was no doctor in town.

All the circumstances combined to make it difficult for Celso, even if he had been versed in dealing with the police, to prove that he was being framed. He was too timid in the face of the all-powerful police authority because he knew from experience that, had he expressed the slightest doubt concerning the proceedings, he would have been given a ten-peso fine for contempt of authority. He only had the right to say yes or no, nothing else. Had he hinted that an agent was after him and that the whole brawl had started just because the agent wanted to get him back on the hook for the monterías, they would only have laughed at him. The fact that he, an Indian, stood accused before the chief of police had scared, confounded and frightened him to such a degree that he did not even try to look at the wound which he was said to have caused.

Obviously his captors had known that he would not dare to question the wound in front of the chief of police. The wound was already many hours old, well dried up by now. The scoundrel had gotten it during a fight in a cantina that same afternoon, not knowing who had done it. But it had been very opportune for Celso's captors. They hired him for fifty centavos to start a brawl with Celso and to show his wound to the police as the result of this fight with Celso.

Celso spent the night in jail. When his captors saw him well guarded, they went to drink aguardiente and then lay down to sleep. They no longer had to watch their prey; the authorities were doing it for them.

Because of the fair there was a lot of business each morning at the police office: brawls, drunkenness, quarrels among the merchants and between the merchants and their customers, petty thefts, small frauds, insults, lack of licenses, counterfeited licenses and concessions, tax frauds and refusals to obey the orders of the authorities. Around noon, it was Celso's turn. His case was very simple. The witnesses were present but interrogation was waived because the police judge knew beforehand how they were going to testify and it would have been a waste of time.

Celso was led to the desk by the two policemen who had arrested him.

"You come from the monterías, Chamula?" asked the police judge.

"Sí, mi jefe, yes."

"How long did you work there?"

"Two years, patroncito."

"For fighting in the street with a dangerous weapon, one hundred pesos fine. Next case."

Celso was pushed before a little desk to one side where the secretary was seated.

"One hundred pesos, Chamula."

"But I haven't got a hundred pesos, patroncito."

"But haven't you worked for two years in the monterías?"

"Sí, patroncito."

"Then you must have at least one hundred pesos."

"But I only have some eighty pesos."

"Well, hand over eighty pesos. For the other twenty pesos and the twenty-five pesos costs of the court, you'll go to jail and earn the money there. Hand over the eighty, Chamula."

Celso had not been searched before. None of the police were interested in knowing what he carried in his pack; as to how much money he had, the police judge would find that out, unless Don Gabriel, the agent, had told him beforehand.

Celso unwound his woolen sash and took out the money, placing it on the little desk. He had about three pesos more than the eighty.

"You can keep those few pesos for the time being, Chamula, to buy tobacco and take care of your other needs while in el bote. Better hurry to get the balance of the fine and you won't have to stay long behind bars."

The secretary was right. Celso did not have to remain for long in the calabozo.

Two hours later Don Gabriel, the agent for the monterías, came in.

He demanded to see Celso. Celso did not know him.

The policemen led Celso to the door and Don Gabriel told him: "I'd like to talk to you, Chamula. Step out here."

Outside, on the street, in front of the police office located in the portico, there was a bench.

Don Gabriel sat down and invited Celso to sit by his side. He offered him a cigarette.

"Won't you have a drink, Chamula?" asked Don Gabriel.

"No, patroncito, gracias, thank you."

"How much of a fine did they sock you?"

"One hundred pesos and twenty-five pesos for costs."

"And how much have you paid?"

"Eighty pesos."

"All you had with you?"

"Almost. I still have a few pesos left."

"For those forty-five pesos which you still owe, the police'll probably keep you here in the calabozo for six months."

"So I believe, patroncito."

Don Gabriel looked up at the sky and then down the street, right and left. A great number of ladinos and Indians roamed the street. To the right one could see part of the plaza where the fair was in full swing. The noise from the market, together with the music played by the itinerant street musicians, the loud talk, laughter and shouts of the happy patrons in the taverns reached their ears. Pack-laden donkeys driven by Indians passed them. An Indian woman drove a group of turkeys to market. People came and went freely in all directions. To the left, steep green mountains rose into the sky. The sun came down from a cloudless, deep-blue sky. High up in the air zopilotes swept their wide graceful circles. Everything looked so free, so easy, so wide open.

For a moment Celso meditated over the six months he would have to spend in jail. The floor was covered with damp bricks. No bed, no cot, no chair, no table. Only walls and a narrow courtyard. Everyone had his petate which he rolled out on the cold brick floor when he wanted to sleep. And all over the place were fleas, bugs, lice, spiders, scorpions, tarantulas, black widows and centipedes ten inches long. And there was so little sun. And there was no green anywhere. Always locked up. Always in a downhearted mood, overwhelmed by homesickness for the wide-open spaces.

In contrast was the jungle, so full of sun, so full of green, of buzzing, ever-changing life. The work is devilish hard, true. But you are out in the open, in the blue shimmering air. At night the sky is over you with all the stars glittering beautifully. Never locked in. Sun, sky, stars, green, humming insects, twittering birds, monkeys playing in the trees, splashing brooks, romantic rivers all the year round. Eternal summer. Clouds of mosquitos, true. The world cannot be perfect. But then few fleas, few lice and no bedbugs. Glorious life in the open.

On the bench, out on the street, sitting with his back against the threatening walled-in jail yard, a montería suddenly seemed to Celso the very image of freedom.

"Mira, muchacho, see here," said Don Gabriel, "you will have to spend six months in this godforsaken calabozo for those forty-five pesos. Money just thrown out in the street. And once you're released again you won't have a single centavito of your own. You know that, of course. Well, muchacho, I'll tell you what I'll do for you. Just for you, see? I'll pay the forty-five pesos for you and in five minutes you'll be out of jail for good. See?"

In five minutes out of jail! For that Celso would, this very minute, have given ten years of his life. And against these ten years which he was willing to sacrifice it seemed like a gift when Don Gabriel told him: "You simply make a new contract for the montería. I'll pay the forty-five pesos, put them down on your account, plus my commission, which will be only twenty-five pesos in your case, and the twenty-five pesos for the tax stamps of the contract. Besides I'll give you right here ten pesos in cash as an advance. So you take up the contract with one hundred and five pesos in your debit account. Once you've worked off those hundred and five pesos all the rest will be clear profit for you."

For a few seconds Celso woke up. During those seconds he became conscious of how long it would take him to work off that advance of one hundred and five pesos. He wriggled undecidedly on the bench.

Don Gabriel was quick in closing the loophole which, he felt, was opening slightly: "There, at least, you'll be out in the open under the sun and the green and you won't have to sleep every night in the piss of some drunk. You'll hear the birds twitter and sing, and occasionally you can hunt yourself an antelope. What have you in this here stinking rat-hole? You can't even drop a crumb of tortilla without the rats fighting over it. And let me tell you something, muchacho, you'll get through that debt quicker than you may think. You're a well-experienced and capable hachero. I'll make out your contract with a daily wage of six reales, seventy-five centavos a day as a generous exception."

Two policemen were dragging in a drunk, kicking him brutally. Celso turned around and saw how the man was thrown upon the floor, kicked again and again, until finally the barred door, made of crude heavy mahogany, was locked after him. He perceived his fellow prisoners looking out on the street with longing eyes from behind the bars of the heavy door.

A policeman stepped up: "Don Gabriel, sorry, I got to take el reo back to jail. Time's up. We haven't anyone here left to watch him. All our men are on duty out on the plaza. Come along, Chamula!"

"El Chamula's coming along with me," Don Gabriel said in a commanding tone. "I'll go in with him to see the clerk."

"You answer for him, then, Don Gabriel?"

"I certainly do. So you leave him to me."

"In that case," the policeman said, "it's all right with me."

Automatically, with no will of his own, Celso followed Don Gabriel into the office. Celso did not know that the sudden appearance of the policeman was part of the game played by Don Gabriel. Celso, dreaming of faraway monterías, had not noticed a significant jerk of Don Gabriel's head in the direction of the policeman.

"I'll pay the balance of the fine for the Chamula," Don Gabriel addressed the clerk. "I'm taking him with me to the monterías."

"Very good, Don Gabriel, good." The clerk hollered at the policeman: "El Chamula esta libre, puede salir."

"Muy bien, jefe," the policeman said, saluting the clerk. He turned and winked an eye at Celso. "Come along, Chamula, fetch your pack. You're free."

When Celso picked up his pack, the policeman told him: "Well, you sure got out of here damn quick. You're very lucky to have found such a good and liberal friend as Don Gabriel who buys you out of this rat-hole. But now see here, Chamula, do you happen to have a duro, a beautiful shiny little silver peso, so that I can take a drink to celebrate your release? Remember I treated you well. I didn't beat you up as I do with all the other junk thrown in here. I didn't search you and take your money away from you as others would've done. After all, that should be worth a silver peso, don't you think? Don Gabriel is liberal. He'll advance you some money."

"Bueno, bueno," said Celso, "you're right, gendarme. Here, take your peso."

"Gracias, gracias, Chamulita, and come back soon." He laughed and corrected himself: "No, of course not, don't come back ever again. You know how I meant it. Buena suerte, good luck in the montería."

Don Gabriel was waiting outside with the contract.

"Got your things, Chamula?" he asked. "Good. Fine. So let's go right away to the Presidente Municipal to sign the contract and put the stamps on."

All the public offices of the locality were in the same building, "el cabildo," the town hall. It was built of adobe. In the main part, facing the plaza, were the offices of the Presidente Municipal, of the Secretary, of the Civil Judge, of the Penal Judge, of the Ayuntamiento or Municipal Council.

Don Gabriel brought Celso before the municipal secretary. Celso could not write. He made a few scrawls on the spot where the secretary put his finger. He recognized as correct the sum advanced for his account and, so as not to leave the slightest doubt, Don Gabriel handed him, before the eyes of the secretary, the promsied advance of ten pesos in cash.

When both stood again on the porch of el cabildo, Don Gabriel told Celso: "You camp with the other men who are going to the monterías. They're camping out there"—Don Gabriel made a vague gesture with his arm—"in that stony plain along the road to the new cemetery. Just ask for Don Gabriel's enganche. The capataces will tell you when we start on the march. You won't run away, will you? I'd get you, even if I had to pull you out of hell. And what awaits you for desertion I need not tell you. You've been in the monterías for two years and so you know the system. Here, take this pack of cigarettes and this package of chicle, so you can move your snout. Off with you and join the gang. Just ask for Don Gabriel's enganche, that's all."

13

 Celso arrived at the camp indicated by Don Gabriel and took off his pack near a fire where he found some men of his own nation, the Tsotsiles.

In jail he had not been given any food. One cannot be bothered with everything; the prisoners were fed when el alcaide, the warden, felt like it, and when there was food. Besides, Celso had no desire to eat. He felt oppressed like a captured deer.

But now, near the fire, where the boys were cooking, eating, talking, chatting and laughing, he gradually recovered his stability and equilibrium.

He began to feel hungry, opened his pack and started pulling out the food which he had bought yesterday for his trip home.

He cut a strip of dried meat and put it in the pan to roast. Then he asked for some water from the kettle of one of his camp fellows and placed his little tin coffeepot near the fire, moving the pan and the little pot from time to time. Frequently he blinked and pressed tears from his eyes because the smoke struck him in the face. Since he was a stranger conversation lagged.

The coffee boiled over and he blew violently into the pot to keep the liquid down. Then he pulled the pot away from the fire but left it close to the ashes to keep it hot.

The meat broiled in the fat poured into the pan from a tin flask. Adding some of the beans cooked the day before, he took a few green chile pods from a rag, cut them into small pieces and threw them into the beans to season them. The tortillas he had were still soft and fresh. He placed them on the hot ashes next to his coffee.

"Any of you ever been in the monterías?" he asked casually, looking up. He had noticed already that all of them were new-comers, and that all they knew about the monterías was what they had been hearing. So he need not have asked. Their an-swer would not have interested him anyway. In fact, he only asked to show those who had built the fire and who, to a cer-tain extent, were his hosts, that he was capable of speech. This question, though he put it a good while after he had squatted down near the fire, he considered as a sort of greeting. And as such it was accepted. The manner in which he had approached the fire and squatted down on his haunches without asking for permission, and the face he had put on, did not encourage any of the boys to start a quarrel with him. He looked as if he were waiting for a reason to knock somebody down. So the fellows, one after the other, said shortly: "No, manito, none of us has yet been in the monterías."

"But I was," he said, watching his coffee, "for two full years. Returned only yesterday."

"And going back to the monterías with us?" asked one.

"Yes, I'm going back with you."

"Then you're going voluntarily this time."

"Exactly as voluntarily as you, nenitos."

As quietly as he had attended to his cooking, he was now eating. Although his entire food made up just about six large spoonfuls, it took him almost an hour to consume it.

In the meanwhile two boys got up, left their packs in charge of a third one and wandered off toward the town where the noise of the festivities was getting louder, nearing its climax which came around seven in the evening.

Celso collected his pans and pots, wiped them clean with a bit of tortilla, packed them back in his net and closed the pack after having taken out a few raw tobacco leaves.

Ceremonially he rolled himself a thick, long cigar, lit it, slid two paces away from the fire, stretched out on the thin grass, drew his pack near him for a headrest and smoked, following with his eyes the slowly dissolving clouds of tobacco. He tried to follow some of the shreds of the smoke as far as he could see. When they vanished, he saw nothing but the open sky.

He felt content, resting there with the assurance of being able to enjoy the sky, the sun, the stars and the green jungle during the coming months. He tossed around a few times on the hard soil and, facing the sky, he thought of the cárcel in which he would have had to spend endless months and months had not Don Gabriel bought him out. Thus quietly resting on the ground, carelessly smoking, his stomach warm from the chile pods, dried meat and beans and the scalding hot coffee, he felt gratitude toward his redeemer, Don Gabriel. Vaguely at first, then clearer and finally forcefully and emphatically, a thought stole into his mind: the thought of his girl and of the fifteen children he hoped to shove into the world with her help. He pulled the cigar from his mouth and sat up with a violent jerk of his body.

"Damn it," he said with a dry throat. "Damn it, God damn it! World of infamous cheating! Two years have passed. She can't wait any longer. She'll be getting old and nobody will want her. Her father can't wait any longer. Not any more. He has given me two years. Two beautiful long years' grace. She can't wait any longer. She'll be too old. She can't wait any more."

By the repetition of his words he tried to understand the situation into which he had slid without once thinking of his girl.

During the whole transaction, he had only thought of the golden sun, the open sky and the green jungle—of that sky, that sun and that green in which, from the moment he was thrown into jail, the girl had formed part. It had been his all-embracing concept of what he considered happiness on earth. The girl and the fifteen children merged into his idea of happiness. But now, with a shock that took his breath away, he realized that the girl and the children had been torn from him, and what was worse, there existed no possibility for him to reweave the torn pieces into a single whole.

When he returned after an additional two years he would find his girl married to another man. It would be hard for him to bear. But far harder would be to read in the faces of the girl and her father the bitter accusation that, for a second time, he had failed to meet his pledge. He had failed twice in his loyalty to the girl, which was equivalent to breaking a solemn marriage vow. In the eyes of his tribesmen, he was a scoundrel to be despised, not only by the girl and her father, but by all the men and women at home. Without their respect it would not be possible for him to live among his people. He would be a pariah, an outcast, a man who had lost his country forever.

The idea of being despised by the members of his clan whom he honored and loved became so unbearable that he thought of dying.

Thinking of death he hit upon a way out which, to him, seemed natural and the only one possible.

Neither now nor ever would he return to his native soil. He would send no news even should there be an opportunity to do so. At home they would believe him dead or lost in the monterías. This way he would preserve what he esteemed highest: the respect of his clan. Voluntarily he would count himself among the dead, among the hundreds of dead working in the monterías. Some day he would die in fact. Perhaps shot by a furious contratista or killed by a fellow worker, or whipped to death by a drunken capataz, or burned up by malaria, or crushed by a prematurely falling trunk of a mahogany tree, or poisoned by the fangs of a snake, or torn to pieces by a jaguar, or drowned when floating trunks or—there are a hundred natural ways to die in a montería. Fate would not deny him this way out to save his honor.

From now on he would no longer care about anything. He would forget the girl, forget her father, forget his fifteen children. He belonged to the dead and so was free to do as he pleased. He could get drunk every day as long as his money lasted. He could lie down with some of the diseased scum back of the church, or under one of the crumbling arches of the old monastery. He could run away, but then he would surely be caught. To avoid the one hundred lashes for desertion he would have to attack his captor and get shot down like a mad dog. He could pick a quarrel with the capataz, talk back and let himself be cut to pieces with a machete. It all came to the same end. He was dead and a man can die only once. Since he had become indifferent to everything he might as well start to make use of the limited freedom which the devil grants the dead.

Not bothering about his pack, which he left unguarded near the fire, he went to the plaza and bought a bottle of aguardiente. Booze is always cheaper by the bottle than by the glass.

He took a heavy gulp, emptying nearly a quarter of the bottle, then offered it to some of the boys lounging around the tienda where he had bought the aguardiente. He took another good mouthful of the fiery stuff.

One hour later he felt like killing someone. He still had enough sense not to seek out Don Gabriel but, with his senses dulled and his judgment limited, he did look for the two hyenas who had delivered him. He would have been satisfied to catch the reptile who had sworn before the police judge that Celso had knifed him in the leg. There was not the slightest doubt that had Celso met those three he would have killed them. But he met none of them. They were either hunting other victims or they had seen Celso very drunk and with a bellicose mien and therefore kept out of his way. He was so hellishly drunk that he could not decide where to go and what to do. So he stumbled, automatically, back to the camp. There he squatted near the fire, talked nonsense, dug stones out of the ground and threw them at the sparse brush nearby.

Then a newcomer arrived at the fire. It was Andrés, who had also been bought by Don Gabriel for the monterías and who now was searching the plain for the groups which belonged to Don Gabriel's enganche. Though Andrés carried a heavy pack Indian fashion, he differed in clothing and hatwear from the Indians who were camping, waiting for their marching orders.

Celso had not been able to cool off his fury by killing his captors. But the newly arrived Andrés looked like a capataz might look. This was the last opportunity for Celso to fight with a capataz and take revenge for everything capataces had done to him and would do in the future. Once on the march it would be too late. Then he would be subject to the cruel law of the montería discipline. But here, on the camping plains, it would be nothing more than an ordinary brawl. The police would sock him a fine of a hundred pesos. And that didn't matter to him. Whether they imposed a fine of ten pesos or of ten thousand pesos would not alter his fate. Don Gabriel would have to pay the fine or lose him. It would be the best punishment that Celso could inflict upon Don Gabriel. And because Celso counted himself among the dead, it was absolutely indifferent to him whether he was to spend two years in the monterías or two hundred years. He had no intention of returning to the living. Therefore, no fine could hurt him, however exorbitant.

He immediately insulted Andrés in the dirtiest way possible and attacked him so violently that, for a moment, it seemed as if Andrés would be finished off for good.

But Andrés was accustomed to hard work just as much as Celso and, although he was dead tired from the long march across the high mountains carrying an unusually heavy pack on his back, he was completely sober while Celso, being almost senselessly drunk, could hardly keep on his feet.

Celso did not last long. The end came quickly and painfully. He called it a draw and stumbled, his face battered, toward the brook, there to act as his own doctor and nurse.

14

 It was late in the evening. The Candelaria fair had
reached the climax of its splendor. Now it would
begin to fade out rapidly. People started to sober up, not only
from drinking, but also from all the merriment, the noise, the
shouting, the bartering and the confusing upheaval. The resi-
dents of the usually quiet and sleepy town were getting tired
of the wild antics of the visitors, the merchants and the mere
pleasure seekers. Longing for their comfortable sobriety, they
had by now become bored with buying and lazily strolling
among the counters, stands and booths. Even the merchants
themselves began to yawn and welcomed the official declaration of the mayor that the fair would terminate on the following evening.

Most of them began to pack their wares and make ready to
leave.

Now the labor agents set about to organize their troops for
the long, tough march through the jungle. The last contracts
were hurriedly confirmed and stamped at the mayor's office.
Don Gabriel displayed still greater zeal in catching a few more
men during the last hours, paying the fines imposed upon them
for drunkenness, scandalizing and disturbing the peace, so that

these unfortunates could be incorporated into the little army of contracted caoba workers before the march began.

There were always a score or so of lost sheep who were remnants of such a wild and crowded festivity—youths who, shamelessly drunk, had gotten into serious trouble or gambled away their last centavo and who now out of desperation ran after the agents begging them to be recruited because nothing mattered to them any more except to make a fast getaway.

So the number of workers increased considerably.

Among these latecomers were many who three days earlier would have been terrified at the mere thought of being hooked for the monterías.

Don Ramón Velasques was the principal promoter, the capitalist of the contracting business which bore his name. He was fairly decent in his dealings as far as decency goes in that rugged enterprise.

Don Gabriel on the other hand knew no limits. Through his stepped-up activity, using uncountable astute tricks, dirty transactions with finqueros, with town clerks, chiefs of police, with judges, with jailers, with wily and alluring promises of the many joys and pleasures presumably found in the monterías, with aguardiente and unasked-for loans of money, he had been able to hook twice as many men as Don Ramón. Nevertheless he was merely Don Ramón's business partner. But now, even before collecting the profit of his hard work, he was resolved to sever his partnership with Don Ramón and to carry on the business for his own account. True, he had a contract with Don Ramón. But what are contracts and agreements if one can grab a better advantage by breaking them? Don Gabriel had already gone so far ahead in his ideas of separating from Don Ramón that he would not have ventured to vouch before the Holy Virgin for the safety of Don Ramón's person. Patiently he was waiting for fate to provide a set of circumstances which would allow him to say to himself that destiny had taken its course or that it had been God's will or that it had just been a stroke of luck. Hundreds of accidents entirely unforeseen and unthinkable can happen on a long march through the tropical jungle.

Already during the previous year Don Gabriel had, as Don Ramón's partner, recruited labor for the monterías, collected them at the Candelaria fair and signed them on in an officially confirmed contract before the authorities in Hucutsin. The situation was generally like this: if a worker under contract did not appear during the Candelaria fair to start his contract, the monterías did not suffer any losses; the agents, the enganchadores, themselves took the responsibility that the laborers contracted would be present at their place of work on a given day. On the other hand, if the monterías ordered their own capataces to take charge of the workers in Hucutsin and march them to the caoba camps, it fell to the monterías to get the men to their jobs. The men who escaped or disappeared or died during the march had to be set down in the books of the monterías as losses, because the recruiting commission had been paid in Hucutsin and the agent had only accepted the risk of handing over the workers in that town during the Candelaria fair.

Although the capataces of the monterías were not exactly shepherds, but rather pretty good executioners and hangmen for the company that employed them, if they lost a man on the march through flight or negligence, the manager of the montería yelled his head off and threatened to deduct the loss of the commission from their salary. But that, of course, was rarely done. After much swearing, hollering and shouting, the case was considered closed and that same evening the capataces would sit peacefully in the company's mess and drink with the other employees of the company. The loss of the missing man would simply be put down in the books of the company as an item of the daily routine.

But if the agent lost men on the march, it was quite a different matter. The company did not pay for those losses. They came out of the agent's pocket. Sometimes a single man would cost the agent two hundred and, not infrequently, three hundred pesos. These were the ransoms, debts and fines paid by the agent to get the man out of jail and hook him. Since the loss of men came out of the agent's pocket, a troop of workers led to the monterías by an agent must not be compared with a smart veterans' parade.

Don Gabriel probably would have severed his partnership with Don Ramón or simply torn up the contract during that same year and devoted himself to the excellent business of recruiting labor to his personal advantage, but he did not know the jungle. He would have been unable to get ten men through unless they went voluntarily. Years ago, when he was younger, he had dealt in cattle and knew how to drive cattle and hogs to market. True, the masses of laborers were driven to the monterías exactly like cattle, but to keep the troop together, one had to know more tricks than those employed in the transportation of animals. Whether the agent liked it or not, occasionally some Indians made use of their human intelligence and disappeared during the march. That some of the more intelligent might instigate mutiny among their fellow workers never occurred to the agent. Whatever the men undertook or thought of undertaking was done individually, everyone for himself and everyone in his own personal way. It would sometimes happen that two would break away in two different directions, and that all the capataces had to ride after the two deserters to catch them. In such a case the troop was practically without supervision. All of them had their chance to run away. The confusion would grow to such an extent that the agents and their drivers would have to catch the men in their native villages with the aid of the police and the rurales. Strange as it may seem, the men seldom took advantage of such confusion. When two or three men broke away and the troop remained without guards, they simply pitched camp where they happened to be, prepared their food and slept until the drivers returned. Not one man more would be missing.

To complete the schooling which Don Gabriel needed to run the business by himself, he still needed the experience of taking a transport of workers to the monterías. Once he had led a transport with as experienced an agent as Don Ramón, he would not need him any longer and would be fully independent in this sort of enterprise. This was the reason why he had so zealously insisted that he and Don Ramón should not deliver the hired men in Hucutsin, but take them instead straight to the monterías themselves. Since it was a matter of a considerably higher profit, Don Ramón was easily persuaded. As a rule, Don Ramón preferred to deliver the workers into the hands of the representative of the monterías in Hucutsin. With the years he had lost some of his former vigor and now disliked the fatigue of such a long march.

15

The march of large groups of workers through the jungle was not at all like the march of a conquering army through unknown territory. This march was shorter, its objectives were known and the road, however poor, could more or less easily be followed by those who knew it. The leader of the transport knew how many days it would take, and he knew all his possibilities of getting supplies or not getting any.

It was a march of men of whom only few went along voluntarily, and of whom none cared a whit for honor or adventure. There was no link of comradeship or any inclination for mutual assistance. All of them were ill-humored and obstinate, and they would not miss an opportunity to cause trouble for the leader of the troop. Everyone felt like a prisoner or galley slave, without hope of a termination of his sentence. Naturally such a march meets with many unforeseen difficulties. The agents who lead those hired men through the jungle need not be strategists. But, in their own way, they have to be outstanding diplomats and experienced tacticians. It won't do for them to shoot a man or to give another one such a hiding that he drops dead on the trail. Each man has to be kept in fairly good shape.

The agents must be capable of settling a quarrel to the satisfaction of all concerned, so that the opponents won't cut each other to pieces and thus constitute a loss of several men for the agent. The agents have to dry the tears of those who are homesick and refuse to eat; otherwise, after three days these men will be so weak that they will perish on the road before they get to the first lakes. To keep the thought of desertion from getting the upper hand, the leaders must convince the men with honey-coated speeches that desertion won't pay, that the fugitive will be caught, no matter if it costs five hundred pesos. They will relate sufficient examples, with names and detailed description, to prove that fugitives are always caught.

The agents must keep the men in good humor. Since the best means of keeping men in good humor is good food, the agents never lose an opportunity to go hunting. The jungle is immensely rich in jabalí, antelope, pheasants and wild turkey, so the agents can easily deliver sufficient fresh meat. For the Indians, who in the misery of their lives in the fincas and in their independent settlements rarely obtain fresh meat, this always offers an occasion for a feast.

Night and day the men on the march are threatened with revolvers or carbines, but there are no shootings. The agent has not spent one or two hundred pesos on a man just to shoot him and leave him for the buzzards. And there is forever the danger that a man who has received a lashing will be unable to march or carry his pack. Or the sores may become infected, and he may get pus-rot or tetanus and die on the road. Then again a man may become as stubborn as an old mule. Then he sits down on the road and cannot be moved by blows or by being pricked with sharp-pointed sticks or with promises of paradise to get up and continue the march. An Indian can fall into such a state of absolute indifference to the surrounding world and all its joys and pains that even if he were told in all seriousness that he could go home, free of all contract obligations, he would refuse to get up and walk. He dies and nothing can save him because he has given up his will to live and, once having given it up, he is unable to recover it.

But just as the revolver and the carbine constantly flash before the marchers' eyes, every minute or so the long whips of the drivers on horseback flick over the heads of the men. That unceasing flicking of whips supposedly is meant only for the pack mules, but it is only natural that an occasional lash will strike the neck, the back or the head of a man. The horseman who brandishes the whip always makes it appear as if he had never intended striking a man and that the blow really had been intended for one of the pack mules or the horse he is riding. The whip simply slipped and struck the neck of one of the boys. The point, however, is that the muchachos are constantly reminded of the fact that the long whip is there.

If a green one receives a blow "by mistake" he will only grumble and mumble; but an old-timer, who has seen more of the world than just his village, immediately heats up: "Hey, you offspring of ten generations of whores, one more blow like that and, damn it all, I'll throw a stone in that dirty snout of yours so that you won't have a single tooth left." Thereafter, even the most arrogant capataz will be flitting his whip with considerably more care, selecting only those who run like rats when he only lifts the whip, for the drivers who, during the days talk big and behave like lion tamers, generally shrink considerably in size when night falls. Night in the jungle is damned black. Sometimes out of a thick bush a knife flashes and lands in the driver's back.

Taking all such incidents into consideration, one arrives at the conclusion that from whatever angle one may judge the labor agents they are clever tacticians and great battalion leaders. To take, with such little help, so many resentful and frequently scheming men through the dense jungle, without getting killed and without losing men through desertion, with a few rare exceptions, requires diplomatic gifts and military skills which are rare even among generals.

The transports were seldom equal in number. It depended upon how many men were needed by the various monterías which asked to be supplied and how many the agent was able to recruit.

This year requirements of labor had been unusually high. A fever epidemic had erased almost four-fifths of the caoba workers. Numerous new concessions for the exploitation of tropical forests had been granted and the concessions about to expire had been renewed. All over the world the demand for mahogany timber was extraordinarily active and prices were steadily growing.

16

    The transport in which Celso and Andrés were
marching consisted of one hundred and ninety contract laborers. In this troop there were youths, very young,
some barely fourteen years old, and also men close to fifty.
Among them there were strong and active men and some were
weak, lazy and clumsy. Many could run like a deer, while
others could only march along slowly like old mules. Some
tired quickly under their packs and had to rest frequently,
whereas others carried their load of eighty pounds as uncon-
cerned as if it were a bag filled with feathers. One of the most
difficult tasks for the agents and the capataces was to keep the
troop close together. The swift must not advance too far ahead
and the weak and unaccustomed must not lag too far behind.
A troop of soldiers is marched easier. Soldiers are approximately all of the same age, of the same physical constitution,
get the same food, are trained all alike and know how to keep
ranks closed. Besides, all carry the same load on their backs.

It required practice to lead such a troop. And it was exactly
this technique which Don Gabriel wanted to learn during this
march. With the troop there came along a caravan of a hundred and thirty mules, all carrying heavy loads of merchandise

to be delivered at the monterías. Don Gabriel and Don Ramón had also bought merchandise which they expected to resell in the monterías at a considerable profit. They had a caravan of their own consisting of thirty-eight mules, all loaded. The animals did not belong to them but had been rented for the march from the arrieros who were leading the caravan. Payment was not according to the number of animals hired but in relation to the weight of the merchandise carried. Thus, they only paid for the freight while the owners and drivers of the animals were sort of a transportation enterprise.

It seemed convenient for certain reasons and inconvenient for other reasons that the two labor agents had allowed the large traders' caravan to join their labor troop. It was inconvenient because at the camping spots not enough fodder would be found for so many animals at the same time. Many of the camping sites lacked pastures and the men had to find and cut leaves off certain trees, the foliage of which the animals accepted for fodder. The more animals came to rest simultaneously at the camp sites, called parajes, the deeper had the arrieros to penetrate the jungle to provide fodder in the needed amounts.

The caravan was taking along sufficient corn. In fact so much that out of each ten pack animals, three did not carry any merchandise but only corn. The mules and horses, however, could not live on corn alone. They were liable to get colics and belly-cramps and might even perish. To have them in good shape for carrying their heavy loads they needed an abundance of fresh green fodder.

For this reason it was inconvenient for the agents to have so many animals along with their troop, because the drivers of the animals who were carrying the trading goods of the agents, had to work too hard and they became bad-tempered. But none of the troops wanted to march two or three days behind the first troop, because in that case the second troop would find all the camping sites barren and deprived of the last miserable little blade of grass. Even with the incredibly fast growth of vegetation in the jungle, it took three weeks or four before sufficient new foliage could be used for fodder.

The parajes were not, as one might think, selected because of a whim of the first caravan leader who marched through the jungle.

In the first place, the camp site has to have water, although frequently it is nothing but a puddle left over from the last rain. Water is not to be found just anywhere in the jungle.

Large stretches of the road are so swampy that it is difficult for the animals to get through. Then again for many miles there are stretches so rocky, so steep and so mountainous that no adequate place can be found to pitch camp. Other parts, for miles and miles, are infested with mosquitos, and others with ferocious large horseflies which madden the animals.

The parajes had been cleverly selected by the first experienced caravan leaders who marched through the jungle guided by Indians. These pioneers learned to know how much of a load their animals could carry and how long each day's march had to be. And that is the reason why each paraje is exactly one day's march from the next for loaded pack animals. But owing to swamps or rocky trails, or because of high mountain passes, some stretches along the road are harder to make than others and so take more time. Therefore certain camp sites, in actual distance as measured in miles, are closer to the next one than others. But as far as marching time is concerned they are all more or less at equal distance.

This limited distribution of parajes inside the jungle is also one of many reasons why a fugitive worker cannot escape smoothly. If his flight is noted and the hunters mounted on horseback are sent after him within thirty hours the fugitive has no chance. Not as long as he is in the jungle. Once out of the jungle he may escape if extremely lucky. Inside the jungle he is bound to a definite trail and to established camp sites. Anyone well acquainted with the jungle will hardly undertake an attempt to run away because he knows that he will probably be caught in three days at the most.

Thus, while pack mule caravans joining a labor troop may spell certain disadvantages for the recruiting agents, they also offer, on the other hand, certain advantages.

The traders and the arrieros of such big caravans are not Indians, not recruited mahogany workers. They are ladinos and some of the mule drivers can perhaps be taken for near-ladinos, so to say. These humans, feeling superior to Indians, increase the general staff and the corps of officers for the agents. They constitute, in every respect, a sort of militia or auxiliary police. Suppose a mutiny breaks out among the workers, the traders and the arrieros form a considerable armed reinforcement for the agents. The traders as well as the leaders of the caravan carry guns in their holsters. Some of the merchants and their assistants carry besides shotguns for hunting.

Throughout the twenty years during which, up to that time, the exploitation of hardwoods in those regions had been carried on, only one serious mutiny had occurred. This mutiny was the basis for many terrifying narrations with which traders and agents passed the time during the long evenings when, in their travels through villages and fincas, they sat with finqueros and rancheros, after supper, on the porches, smoking, swinging in rocking-chairs or lounging in hammocks.

17

Don Anselmo Espíndola was a capable and experienced agent. He had received a commission to recruit from twenty to twenty-five men, Indians of course, and to take them to the montería Los Zendales. He had bought only six from fincas because he lacked the necessary funds to pay off the high debts of the others.

He came to the region of the Bachajones, who lived in independent villages and settlements. There he collected some twenty men who, for some reason or other, needed ready cash and had no prospect of getting it except by signing a contract to work for one year in a montería.

Don Anselmo had not been able to wait for the Candelaria fair to march with a larger troop and in the company of other agents. By agreement, he had to deliver his men at once to their future working place.

A boy of about fourteen was to serve him as a sort of assistant.

Labor agents, though ruthless in their trade of tricking and buying up Indians, are men whom only this country can produce. An agent does not know the meaning of fear. Not a muscle in his face will move if somebody pushes a loaded gun into his ribs or if he wakes up and finds somebody standing over him with the point of a machete at his throat. But while he has no fear, he is certainly not brave in the accepted sense of the word. Rather, he is completely indifferent to the value of life. The agent looks into the bore of a gun and says to himself: "Pues, mi hora ha llegado, my hour has come, and there is nothing that can be done about it." This, however, does not in the least mean that he will not fight. If he sees a possibility, he will defend himself to the last breath. If he is so cut to pieces that there is no hope of saving his life, he'll keep on fighting; now no longer to save anything, but to take revenge so that his opponent won't leave as healthy as he came. Should he, at the moment of his death, perceive that his antagonist is also dying, he won't accept a reconciliation to gain a seat in Heaven. He has won his paradise once he sees his adversary die half a minute earlier than himself.

Don Anselmo was no exception to this type.

The twenty-six Indios, going more or less against their will to the monterías, were, owing to the separation from their families, in the worst imaginable temper. Bachajones belonged to an independent tribe whose members were well known as proud, obstinate, quarrelsome men, always ready to attack, men who would never fully submit to anyone, not even to established authority. To drive Bachajones for twelve to fifteen days alone through the jungle was a task which no ordinary man would have had the audacity to undertake. Nobody familiar with the conditions would have called any man a coward who refused the chore. Don Anselmo had accepted the commission without flicking an eyebrow, which in itself proved that he was no ordinary man. He knew the road and knew the men he was leading —their reputation, their strong character. He told himself: "If I get these men through, I'll make a fair pile of money. If I fail, well, the buzzards will pick my bones, in company with the wild pigs and red ants. Suppose I take on three men as drivers;

there won't be much profit left. So, whether I like it or not, I got to go alone with this little chit of a youngster and see how matters come off."

The three days' march to the little ranch where jungle travelers obtained their necessary supplies passed without incident. Nevertheless, Don Anselmo heard mutterings, and noticed that the muchachos fought with one another. After each period of rest, the getting up and making ready to continue the march was accompanied by gestures of laziness and with visible unwillingness. Grumbling grew more frequent than was usual on such a march.

But he consoled himself with the thought that, once in the jungle, humor would improve. There the men would not meet any acquaintances; there would be no huts inhabited by Indian peasants or ranch hands to remind them of home. They would fall into the sort of stupor typical of soldiers on forced campaign marches, who trot along without thinking any more of why they march, where they march or how long they are going to march. They arrive at a state of mind in which they will even march for hours in a circle without realizing it.

Don Anselmo knew that the men, with heavy packs on their backs and constantly under the influence of the same surroundings, now marching, now resting, now up again to continue marching, after a few days would become utterly depressed because of this monotony which deprived them of all power to think beyond a single question: When do we reach the next camp site?

They marched in a long single file, one after the other. The narrow trail did not permit any other formation.

Don Anselmo had two mules which carried his own necessities and those of the boy, together with food for both, plus corn for his own horse, that of the boy and for the two pack mules themselves.

The boy rode at the head of the group. He was followed by the pack mules and, after them, Don Anselmo.

About twice every hour and wherever the path allowed it, Don Anselmo stopped his horse, dismounted, tightened the saddle girths, stood against a tree, lit a cigarette, slowly mounted again and followed the troop. He gave this action the appearance of a desire to stretch his legs. But, in fact, he did it to let the whole troop pass by so that he might count and see that nobody lagged behind.

The fact that a man remained behind did not necessarily imply an attempt to desert. It might have been the need to take something out of his pack, or to change the arrangement of his pack to distribute the load differently; or he might have stubbed his bare toe against a rock, or felt the need of going behind a tree, or wanted to roll himself a cigar. There were scores of plausible explanations. If a man was missing, Don Anselmo waited for a while. When the man did not come along he rode back to see what had become of him. When he found him and saw that the man had a reason for lagging behind, he would shout at him: "Hey, you, que pasó, what happened? A thorn in your foot? Let's see. Wait, I'll pull it out. Now, on your way and hustle. The others are far ahead. Come on, come on!"

If somebody was really missing once camp had been pitched, Don Anselmo had to mount his horse again and look for the man. It could have happened that he had hurt himself and was unable to walk.

The fourth day was unusually hot. The men seemed very tired. Owing to the heat and the heavy humid air, the march presented great difficulties while crossing steep mountain ridges. At each brook they squatted down, cooled their necks, took out their gourds and drank. Most of them did not merely drink but kneaded a piece of pozol in the water to make the drink more refreshing and give it, at the same time, considerable nourishment value.

For a while Don Anselmo did not comment on these rather frequent stops.

But when, within two hours, they stopped for the third time, took off their packs and delayed the march, he shouted angrily: "Hey, muchachos, esto no sirve pa' nada. This won't do. If we continue like this, we won't reach camp today. You know damned well we can't camp in a swamp. We got to make the next paraje. Get up. Get going."

One of the men mumbled something in Tseltsal. Don Anselmo had the sense of a diplomat not to ask him what he meant. A few of the boys acted as though they hadn't heard what Don Anselmo had said. Phlegmatically they continued to knead pozol in their jícaras and took all the time in the world before packing up again. So clumsily did they do it that one might wonder if they had ever known how to pack. The majority, however, got up rapidly, took up their packs and were already marching while the rest still squatted by the brook, rinsing their gourds.

Even after the march had been progressing for quite a while Don Anselmo remained in the rear to see that nobody was missing. When he caught up again he noticed that the muchachos were unusually quiet. No one spoke. Since all of them were barefoot they marched in absolute silence. The only noise that Don Anselmo could hear was the squeaking of his own saddle and the groaning and rustling of the packs on the backs of the mules.

And now, for the first time in his life, Don Anselmo was afraid. Suddenly it dawned upon him that he had placed himself in a most dangerous situation. He thought of the many things which might happen to him any minute now. Suppose the men started a mutiny. For the first time he fully realized that he was alone in the depths of the jungle with a large group of Bachajon Indians who, because of their rebellious nature, had the worst reputation in the whole state. They certainly had not the slightest interest whatever in his life or in his well-being. On the contrary, they had no wish whatever to see him alive and happy. He knew that he was completely defenseless and at their mercy. He was a good enough marksman to shoot six of them, but the twenty left alive would not give him time to recharge his gun.

When his thoughts reached this point a sudden terror overcame him. What if he had lost his gun? What if one of the men had picked it up? That most likely was the reason why they had been so obstinate at the brook and why one of them had even started to grumble aloud, with no respect at all for him. With a rapid movement his hand went back to find the heavy grip of his revolver.

Drawing the gun from the holster, while casually riding on, he made sure the chambers were loaded and the safety catch was working. He pushed the gun back into its holster and lit a cigarette.

But several men marching behind him had seen his hasty movement in search of the gun. They looked at one another. Wide grins appeared on some faces. Don Anselmo's anxious checking of the weapon had betrayed something which he had hoped to keep hidden for all eternity: that he could be afraid.

At the next brook, when the men rested again, he did not say a word. He let them do as they pleased. He, too, prepared his pozol Indian fashion but added a little sugar from a tin box to make the drink more appetizing.

Half an hour later the troop arrived at a river which had been named Las Tazas, The Cups, because of a queer formation of the stones in the river bed.

When the men again took off their packs and pulled out their jícaras, thus giving the impression that they intended to take another rest, not at all needed after so short a time, Don Anselmo became really infuriated.

In a shrieking voice he yelled: "Hey, you lousy bastards, get up and move on or by God Almighty we'll never arrive at the monterías before All Saints Day. Up, up! Abran las piernas! I'll tell you where and when to rest!"

He had stopped his horse in the middle of the river. The pack mules and the boy on horseback had already climbed the opposite bank and were trotting into the thick of the jungle without glancing back. The animals had not halted to drink because they had been sipping up water abundantly during the frequent rests of the troop.

Don Anselmo had transported Indian workers long enough to learn when and how often they must drink and mix their pozol to remain fit. Now this day was very hot, true. But an Indian can march for hours in much greater heat without whining for water. It would never have occurred to Don Anselmo to prevent the men from refreshing themselves when they came to a brook or a river, just as he would not have prevented his mules and horses from drinking.

What infuriated him was the fact that during the last three hours the men had at each watercourse made a real rest pause such as should be made only twice during a whole day's march if one intends to arrive at the established paraje before night sets in.

One Bachajon, who sat on one of the stone cups in the water, yelled, with the same shrieking voice Don Anselmo had used: "You goddamned blasphemous dog of a ruthless devil, who are you to deny a poor nearly dying Indito a drink of the water which has been placed here in our road by the good God in Heaven? To hell and all its torments with you, you heathen offspring of a filthy, lousy whore."

That an Indian, a peon, should dare shout something like that to a ladino was utterly incredible. Even if a peon was blind drunk from the worst aguardiente squeezed from an unlicensed still, he would never say anything like that. Not to a ladino. Bachajones, however, were not peons; they were free men from an independent Indian community, recognizing as their authority only the chieftains elected by them.

Like a flash it came to Don Anselmo that there must be some aguardiente, some real firewater, in the troop. In no other way could he explain the attitude of the men.

Generally, during the first two days of a march, there was some aguardiente in the packs, though it was used up so fast and so thoroughly that on the evening of the second day there seldom remained enough to get anybody drunk.

Whether some of the men might be drunk or not, was now beside the point. The mood was there and Don Anselmo realized that a mutiny was under way.

The boy leading the pack mules had already advanced a good distance ahead of the troop. For a fraction of a second Don Anselmo thought of whistling or calling him back. Yet at the same instant he decided it would be better to let the boy continue on his way. If he called him back and matters became really serious, he, too, would be killed. And Don Anselmo considered that a needless sacrifice.

Within three seconds a hundred plans, most of them utterly silly, flashed through his head.

He did not know whether he could count upon a single one of the men to stand by him. The six peons he had bought from a finca where they were indebted seemed to be safe to a certain extent. They would not attack him. They had too deep rooted a respect for a ladino. But he did not believe he could count on any of the Bachajones. Even if there were some among them not exactly hostile, they would not come to his assistance, being afraid of those who now seemed to be in command of the situation.

However, Don Anselmo had not sufficient time to ponder all these possibilities calmly and to arrive at a logical conclusion. Action would not wait for the result of his thoughts. He had not even enough time to establish, by a look around him, who were his enemies and who were neutral.

He was sitting on his horse in the middle of the river. Since some of the men had already been on the opposite bank of the river while others had kept in the rear, they now held both banks. Not only that, but several sat on the cups, those strange stone formations in the river.

At this section the river was not very deep, and therefore it had been forded here for the last forty years or so by caravans headed for the mahogany camps. The water came just below the hips of the men. By jumping from one cup to the next, one could cross the river at this point without even getting his calves wet.

Don Anselmo was completely cornered. All had happened so rapidly and unexpectedly that he only noticed it when there was no escape left. Nothing would help him now, not even a bold jump with his horse. The cups were distributed so unevenly in the river bed that, wherever the horse jumped to reach the opposite bank, it surely would fall and probably break a leg. Horses and mules had to ford the river very cautiously to avoid accidents.

With a fast move Don Anselmo drew his gun. He had no intention of training his gun on the man who had reviled him, and he didn't mean to shoot anybody. That would have done him no good whatever. He only drew his gun to have it ready in his hand and defend himself against his closest aggressor. Then if he reached the opposite bank he could ride a stretch and so gain time to think out a plan or just wait until the men came to their senses and quieted down.

18

 Yet everything turned out differently from what he had calculated.

At the same time that he drew his gun his horse received a powerful blow on the rump with the broad side of a machete from one of the men who had jumped from a cup and landed close to the horse.

Because of the unexpected blow the horse reared up. And because the rider had not expected this, he slid down backward into the water.

Immediately he got up, pushing and dragging himself to the nearest cup. While he was stepping up on the side of the cup to be able to stand firmly on it and jump from there over a few more cups to the bank, one of the men leaped off the opposite cup and with a long stride passed over to the same cup which Don Anselmo was trying to reach. The Indian hit him a blow with the sharp edge of his machete straight across the face. Then another Indian came from behind and struck Don Anselmo a terrific blow on the right shoulder. The blow had been aimed at the head. If it had landed true that would have been the end of the fight. But while dragging himself up to the cup Don Anselmo had bent his head to one side precisely at the same instant that the blow was delivered. Yet even landing on the shoulder it would have sufficed to finish him off. Fortunately for him, however, he was wearing a leather pouch, a so-called morral, slung from a thick, broad strap over his right shoulder, and by the movement of his efforts to pull himself up, the strong iron buckle for lengthening or shortening the strap had slipped on top of the shoulder.

As a result this second blow caused him only a slight cut.

Don Anselmo did not whimper for mercy. He didn't beg anybody not to murder the father of his children and the provider of his family. He was too good a Mexican for that. Before the two men could raise their machetes again and begin cutting him to pieces, he pulled his torso completely up on the cup and dealt the Indian who had slashed his face such a blow with the barrel of his gun against the kneecap that the man was going to be harmless for a good while.

Another pull brought Don Anselmo fully on the cup. But he did not stand up because he knew that one of the men was behind him. He did not actually see him but he had felt the man's blow on his shoulder. As soon as he gained the top of the cup, he quickly twisted around and with his heavy spurred boot delivered such a savage kick in the groin of the man that he bent over with a yell of pain, slipped off the cup and writhed around in the water like a wounded alligator.

He, too, would be harmless for a few hours.

Indians, although by nature highly intelligent, have, as a rule, little experience for organization. The Bachajones, true to their race, did not know how to organize the situation they had created to their advantage. Unable to keep the final end in view, all those who had not actively participated in the fight simply sat where they had been sitting before the struggle started. They looked on passively as if it were a pantomime in a circus.

Four hundred years ago, this lack of talent for organization and intelligent planning had allowed the fiendish bandit and soulless cutthroat Cortés to slip out of a hopeless situation. Now it allowed Don Anselmo to escape with his life. Only one or two of the other men who were squatting around watching the fight as if it did not concern them in the least had to get up, grab a stone and throw it at Don Anselmo's head. With one of the thick branches floating in the river the weakest of the muchachos could have killed him. If one of them had had the sense to yell: "Now, come on, let's finish him," that would have signaled the end.

But nobody did anything. The two who had launched the attack were now worrying about themselves. They did not think of attempting a second attack. And the old feeling of submission, of obedience and respect for the ladino rapidly regained its hold on their minds. They turned completely humble. By just wiggling his finger Don Anselmo could have ordered any of them, even his two attackers, to come close. And the man would have come, saying in a sheepish way: "A sus órdenes, patroncito, at your service."

Though Don Anselmo knew that he had the situation well under control and that by now he could be more certain than ever of getting the troop to the montería, he was not yet ready to resume command.

The slash he had received across his face was keeping him low. His forehead was opened, the nose cut, one cheek parted down to the chin, baring his teeth. Thick blood ran down his face, so that he could hardly see. He bathed his head in the river, but the blood wouldn't stop. At this moment he was absolutely unable to defend himself.

He pulled himself up to the bank and began to dip his bandanna into the water to wash his face, wringing it out and repeating this operation several times.

19

 Don Anselmo kneeled on the river bank, soaked to the skin, bathing and cooling the open wound in his face. He was dead tired and had no will left to offer any resistance. Had any of the men beaten him with a heavy wet rag he would have keeled over like a rotten tree.

All around him, on both banks and on several cups in the river, the victors squatted. Some, not knowing what else to do, again prepared their pozol. Others busied themselves with their packs. And still others picked sand fleas from their toes or searched their legs, arms and naked torsos for those infinitely small prickles that rubbed off in the jungle from certain plants, so small that one can hardly see them, but nevertheless very painful and uncomfortable. Nobody bothered about the two men who had attacked Don Anselmo and who were now nursing themselves, one his kneecap and the other his groin.

There the Indians squatted, indecision in their every gesture, indecision in their low conversation as though they were afraid of waking somebody. And there was indecision even in their sideway glances toward Don Anselmo. They were the victors all right, but they did not know what to do with their victory. They could go back to their villages. Nobody would prevent them from doing so. If at this moment they gave Don Anselmo the final blow and buried him, not even the police would be after them for breach of contract, because there would be no plaintiff to press the case. And if they wanted to, after burying Don Anselmo, they could all march to the montería as volunteers. Since there would no longer be an agent to demand from the montería administration the advances given them, they would receive their full pay and, after two years, would return home with a handsome sum of money.

None of them were obligated to know what had happened to Don Anselmo. They were not his bodyguard. The boy who traveled along with the troop as Don Anselmo's personal servant had seen nothing, because he was riding a long way ahead. The muchachos would make up a tale about Don Anselmo having seen a herd of jabalíes which he had followed to shoot one or two for fresh meat. The men had waited on the trail for an entire day and night, but he never came back. "Probably," they could say, "the wild pigs knocked him down and then ate him while he was still half alive." Or he might have fallen prey to a cougar, crouching on a tree under which Don Anselmo happened to pass. He also could have been bitten by a snake and perished in the depths of the jungle. Any of the hundreds of causes which may mean death for a human being in the jungle might have occurred. All they had to do was to agree on the same story. Instead they sat on their hams, waiting to see what would happen next.

Three of the men who had stopped on the same river bank where Don Anselmo knelt began a low-voiced discussion. Then they went to fetch green leaves from certain plants which they selected very carefully. Finally they approached Don Anselmo.

When he saw them come straight toward him, he reached for the gun lying by his side. Quite naturally he thought the three were coming to finish him off. If he had to die he, as a true Mexican, was not the kind to take it lying down like a sick dog.

He was resolved to take at least as many with him to hell as he could get in his last moment.

Aim carefully he could not because his hand was trembling owing to his great weakness. But he still managed to train his gun fairly well on the men.

He pulled the trigger. But the gun only went "pfish." He pulled the trigger a second time and now the gun went "pfut."

Don Anselmo let go with the most awful blasphemies against all the saints, appealed to the devil and to all the damnations he had ever heard of and, in the same breath, asked the saints and the Virgin to strike all ammunition makers on earth with small-pox, syphilis and cancer because they made such lousy stuff that an honest Mexican couldn't even fall into a river without finding himself defenseless in front of his enemies.

The men watching him had noticed that on two successive occasions the gun failed to go off. Thus they realized once more that he was completely in their hands. They didn't even need a club to liberate him from all his pains and further wor-ries. A hard kick with a foot against his head would have sufficed to roll him into the river where he would drown.

But the men did nothing. They just squatted and looked with interest at the whole scene like people watching a show.

Without betraying by the slightest gesture that there was anything wrong with his gun, Don Anselmo opened the drum in a very businesslike manner, expelled the cartridges, threw them into the river shrieking: "Que chin—a sus madres y abuelas!" at the ammunition makers, extracted new cartridges from his belt and pushed them into the drum. He snapped the drum back into place, threw the gun up into the air so that it made two somersaults, deftly caught it again by the grip and pushed it back into the holster with an energetic gesture. He knew perfectly well that this reloading of the gun did not arm him again because the cartridges in the belt were just as soaked as those in the drum, if not more, because those inside the drum had, at least in part, been protected. But the showy manipulation was smart. He knew the men used only old muzzle-loaders for hunting and would, therefore, not know that the cartridges taken from the belt were not a whit more effective than those Don Anselmo had thrown into the river. It was nothing but a very hoary strategem, not unlike a hundred similar ones by which wars have been won and more rebellions lost than historians have recorded.

The men who had been approaching Don Anselmo with branches and leaves in their hands had stopped in their tracks when Don Anselmo pulled the gun—whether out of courage or out of indifference would be hard to say, because they knew that running away is not much good against flying revolver bullets.

That the gun failed to go off did not impress them. At least they showed no surprise. They let Don Anselmo reload, watching him from where they had stopped when he aimed his gun at them.

Once he had pushed his gun back into the holster, one of them said in a loud voice: "Patroncito, we only want to bring you hierbas buenas, some healing leaves, to cure your wound and stanch the blood. Understand, you may bleed to death right here, patroncito."

"Bueno, bueno, muchachos," said Don Anselmo, while wringing out his bandanna in the water, "come on, bring the curitas and let's see if they are any good."

The muchachos came close, picked up stones, dipped them into the water to wash off the earth and then ground and stamped the leaves and thin twigs into a sort of pulp. They helped Don Anselmo to put the mush on his wound and to tie it up firmly with his bright-colored bandanna. Once bandaged, he turned first left and then right and said: "Goddamn it, where is that maldito cabrón, that horse of mine?"

"El caballito está detrás de las otras bestias ya bien adelante en el camino," said one of the muchachos.

"Well, if it is ahead already I suppose I have to make it on foot to the next paraje," said Don Anselmo, clumsily trying to get up.

As soon as he stood on his feet he wavered, but he got hold of himself, stumbled with two long, dragging strides toward a tree and leaned against it. He shook himself like a wet dog. Then he let off steam, swearing in the most blasphemous way, berating the saints, the federal government and that of the state, and in particular the poor condition of business which forced him to take up such a godforsaken profession, that of giving work and bread to miserable Indians, whom he, out of sheer generosity, freed of their debts and bondage. Then he shouted: "Hey, you whoring bastards, cabrones y ladrones malditos, has none of you a drop of goddamn stinking aguardiente or comiteco? Whatever it is, hand it over!"

One of the men still squatitng on one of the cups replied: "Tenga, patroncito. I've got a bottle."

"Of course, I knew it, puercos, marranos del diablo, I knew that some of you goddamned swine would drag a bottle along. That the Santísima Madre del Dios Poderoso slay you and rot your filthy bones. I knew there was booze in the outfit. Hand over the stuff."

The man pulled a bottle out of his pack, jumped from cup to cup across the river and offered the fifth, more than half full, to Don Anselmo.

Don Anselmo screwed out the corncob which served as a cork, smelled the contents, sniffed noisily, smelled again, sniffed more noisily than before and yelled at the top of his voice: "I should've known it. It's Doña Emilia's piss. That old goddamn hag isn't satisfied with keeping a whore house with half a dozen bitches, every one of them ten times a grandmother and fatter than a prize sow. No, she has to brew booze on top of it.

Only God Almighty knows what that lewd slattern has spit and pissed into her bottles this time."

He lifted up the bottle, stared at it, made a gesture as if overcome by nausea and took a huge gulp. He shook himself with all his might, belched terribly and spat out the stuff that still lingered in his mouth in a wide curve against the bushes lining the river bank. He yelled: "That I, an honest and faithful Catholic, should have to drink such goddamned whore's piss when I can hardly stand on my feet no one would believe. That damned old whoring bitch should be hanged for brewing this stinking stuff, and she even has the nerve to call it 'comiteco añejo.' No wonder that with such rotgut in their belly the boys go crazy and think of murder. I would do the same." Shaking himself wildly he took still another swallow out of the bottle. Then, the bottle swinging in his hand, he broke out in another stream of oaths.

However, he did not do this just to entertain the boys, who by now only stared at him in deep silence. They did not even mumble among themselves. They only watched him to see what he might do. But his swearing only proved that he was slowly becoming himself again. He had to get his mind clear and off the fact that only a few minutes before he had been as near to death as any human being can come. Besides, he had to dull the terrific pain which now, since the shock was over, increased so much that he thought he could not bear it any more without going insane. A severely wounded, dying soldier who in his agony swears the blue out of the skies and the saints out of Heaven feels in his heart that he is more assured of the understanding of Nature's God than the mollycoddle who whines for a soul-saver's babblings, which to the dying soldier are utterly meaningless. If you have to go to hell, do it with dignity like a man and don't bother about trifles which won't change the outcome anyway.

With a horrified grimace on his face Don Anselmo looked

critically at the bottle in his hand, and when he noticed that less than one-third of its contents was left he gave it back to its owner and said: "Gracias. But let me tell you, son, if you don't want to die poisoned but return to your mother someday instead, don't take another drop of this stuff."

At this the boy grasped the bottle, went to his pack and stored it very carefully away between a pair of pants and his woolen blanket.

"Hey you, come here," Don Anselmo called the boy back. Taking him aside so that the other boys should not overhear their conversation, he reached into his pocket, produced a small leather purse, fumbled in it for a coin and said: "There, take this tostón for the aguardiente I drank out of your bottle, for which sin only God Almighty in person can forgive me."

He searched his shirt pocket for cigarettes. He pulled out a package which was nothing but a brown mealy paste in soaked and dissolving paper.

"I've got cigarettes, patroncito," said one of the men, getting up from the ground and coming near. He only had the type which is very good uncured tobacco wrapped in ordinary packing paper. This coarse paper does not exactly contribute to the pleasure of smoking. "But then what can you do if you haven't got something better," thought Don Anselmo to himself.

He took the cigarettes offered him. "Tonight, at the paraje where we camp, I'll give you a whole new package. Good ones. I've got plenty in my packs."

"Gracias, jefecito," said the man. "Shall I look for the caballito and bring it back, patroncito?"

"No, let it go. The horse is along with the other animals by now and too far ahead. Before you're back, night will have fallen. I'll march on foot like all of you. Good for my health." And so saying he lit a cigarette, took a few puffs, then he shouted: "Oigan, muchachos, let's be on our way. Get up.

Come on, damn it all, we got to make the next paraje or sleep on the road like pigs. Abran las piernas. Get going."

Without waiting to see whether all the men would really follow, he pulled up his pants, tightened his belt and as, owing to his bandage, he couldn't put his hat on straight, he slapped it on sideways and started on his way.

20

It was tough going at first. He wobbled along, swayed and had to rest leaning against a tree now and then to gain new strength. After half an hour he went on better. By now he had really found his stride. Not once did he turn around to look back. He left it entirely to the men whether they wanted to follow or complete the mutiny and return home.

The next paraje was at a distance which on a regular march could have been reached about four in the afternoon, the hour most preferred by jungle travelers.

Don Anselmo arrived between six and seven o'clock. Sunset was close.

His boy had been worrying because he had not seen anyone for hours. But since he had left the entire troop including the boss behind, he hoped that everything would turn out normally. He was not particularly surprised when Don Anselmo's horse came trotting along by itself and was wildly greeted by the other animals at the camp with snorts, braying and neighing.

Two hours later, when neither Don Anselmo nor any of the muchachos had showed up, the boy became restless. But there

139

was nothing he could do. If he mounted his horse and rode back, the other animals left alone would stray away. He told himself that since Don Anselmo was in the company of more than twenty men, they would surely bring him to the camp if anything happened to him. After waiting undecidedly some time, the boy unloaded the mules, unsaddled the horses, let them roll around on the ground and then had them look for fodder. Fixing up the camp as well as he could, he built a fire and began to prepare the usual meal, consisting of beans, rice and dried meat. When the coffee was boiling Don Anselmo arrived and let himself drop close to the fire, dog tired. The boy pushed a saddle behind Don Anselmo's back so that he could rest against it and offered him coffee, and hot beans and rice, mixed in a pan.

"Que pasó, jefe? Anything happen to you?" asked the boy. Don Anselmo drank the scalding coffee, shoved a few hard toasted tortillas close to the fire and said: "Nothing that matters. Not even worth discussing it. Some of the muchachos got drunk. I got a blow with a machete over the head. That's all. Don't know who did it. Doesn't matter anyhow. You know how such things happen. And so while I was washing off the blood, the horse made off by itself. That's why we're late. Eso es todo. Nada en particular."

"Didn't you shoot, Don Anselmo?" asked the boy.

"I wasn't drunk, so why shoot? What do you think, chamaquito? Why shoot? I'd only shoot up my own good money. And I'm not that loco, to amuse myself by shooting my own money to pieces. Come on, open a can of sardines. I just feel like celebrating. Do we still have any comiteco left in the bottle?"

"More than half full," replied the boy. "Do you want the bottle now, Don Anselmo?"

"Not right now. Later. After supper. Before lying down.

Give me those sardines. Where's the salt? Any of the mules saddle galled?"

"No, jefe, the mules are in fine shape. No sore backs."

"You were not afraid all by yourself, chamaquito? Or were you?"

"I'm no coward. I was only worried that something might have happened to you. Perhaps with the muchachos."

Don Anselmo laughed. "You needn't worry about me. You ought to know that. And the muchachos are good boys, all of them. No exception. Just homesick, that's what they are."

"Pues," the boy replied, "I'm not so sure about the Bachajones. Son matones. Killers. But look, patrón, there they're coming."

Don Anselmo looked toward the point where the trail ran into the paraje. The men were arriving, one by one, single file.

Darkness settled quickly. Before the last of the men arrived night had closed in completely.

At the camp one could only see the dancing fire and the men, moving about like shadows.

They built their own fires, several of them, away from Don Anselmo's.

Don Anselmo did not know whether all the men were present, and if not, whether they would arrive later, perhaps on the following day, or never.

Long before sunrise on the next morning the camp was busy. Some of the men went out to fetch the scattered animals and helped to load them. It was not their job but they did it anyway.

When they were ready to march all the fires were extinguished, stamped down and covered with earth. Don Anselmo, already in the saddle, shouted: "On our way, muchachos! Vamonos!"

As soon as they took the trail Don Anselmo told the boy to

ride ahead to guide the animals. He himself followed, without bothering to count the men in the troop.

His wound hurt him considerably. He had not taken off the bandage during the night. It was sticking strongly to his skin, and whenever he made a careless movement with his head, the bandage tore at the wound and increased the pain. In the evening, he had examined the short wound on his shoulder as best as he could. It was only about a finger long and half an inch deep. He did not attach any importance to it. Such a little scratch was not worth thinking of. He poured some comiteco into the cut. Not much. Just a little. It was too valuable to waste on a wound.

Three days later the troop arrived at the montería, and at last Don Anselmo found it necessary to count the men he had brought along. He had lost only two—the two Bachajones who had attacked him. He brought no complaint against them and did not have them pursued for breach of contract on which they had been given a considerable advance to pay off their debts. He simply considered them losses in the same way as if they had died on the march.

In the montería he was asked how he had gotten his wounds. He said that one of the men had hit him with a machete and then run away. He did not go into details. In due time, however, the circumstances of the case became known, because some of the men told them to fellow workers at the montería.

A well-known citizen of Jovel by the name of Don Anselmo carries his scar to this very day. It is so noticeable that nobody can help seeing it, for he can't cover it up. If someone who doesn't know him is looking for him, he is told: "Oh, you mean Don Anselmo with the big red scar all over his face. You can't mistake him for any other Don Anselmo."

Today Don Anselmo is still a recruiting agent. Dozens of times since that eventful march he has led half a hundred Indians through the big jungle to the monterías, accompanied only by a boy to save expenses. He doesn't do it for pleasure or for adventure. No. He has to support a steadily growing family. It is the only trade he knows and it gives him a sufficient income to keep his family fed, clothed and housed.

Every time he thinks that the youngest girl has passed the worst and that now he will be able to purchase a small store and spend the rest of his life quietly in the comfortable neighborliness of a small town, his wife says to him: "Anselmo, you know, I think the next one is going to be a boy." So what can he do? He must go out again and contract workers and get them to the monterías. He is tied by exactly the same rope from which the men whom he recruits for the mahogany companies hang; and if he does not use his head better than do the Indians whom he takes there, it might happen that he won't come to the monterías as the recruiting agent, but as a contracted laborer sold to the montería for his debts.

21

 People who fight at their first meeting often become the best of friends.

Thus it happened to Andrés and Celso. When Celso sobered up enough to look at the surrounding world clearly, he made his peace with Andrés. But he made it clear to Andrés that the cause of the encounter had been Andrés fault as much as his own.

Through his long years of working as a carretero on the highways of the state, Andrés had lost almost completely the customs and the manner of speech of the Indians that hailed from the little independent villages as well as those of the peons belonging to the fincas. Through his way of dressing and because of his permanent contact with ladinos and, even more, through the fact that he had learned to read and write, Andrés gave the impression that he was of that class from which the monterías and the coffee plantations selected their capataces and privileged workers, the so-called "empleados de confianza," whom they needed because of the degree of education which they had been able to acquire.

It was therefore only natural that Celso should see in Andrés, when the latter arrived at the camp of the future caoba workers, a capataz, a spy, a driver and a stoolpigeon. And because the fury which Celso felt against capataces, drivers and henchmen had reached its climax, it was in many ways excusable that he should have attacked Andrés without apparent cause. Once he knew Celso's story, Andrés understood Celso's rage better than many others would have. He himself, like Celso, through no fault of his own and without being able to do anything about it, had fallen into the clutches of a contracting agent, the same Don Gabriel.

Owing to a number of different circumstances, Andrés had been separated from the finca, of which, like the cattle and the land, he was a part. But though the finqueros, at times, may apparently let a peon go his own way, whenever they believe it to be to their advantage, they will find a way to get the peon back when they think they need him again.

On the finca from which Andrés came, there lived his father, his mother and his younger brothers and sisters. Andrés' father, born on the finca like his grandfather before him, was indebted to the finquero. The finquero, afraid that Andrés' father might die before he could work off his debts, decided to collect by selling him to Don Gabriel for the amount of the debt. Andrés' father was getting on in years and probably would no longer be taken on as a fully capable caoba man. The finquero pointed this out to the agent, Don Gabriel, but he put Don Gabriel's mind at ease on the matter: "Don't worry, Don Gabriel. You won't have to take the old man. You'll get the young one, his boy, strong and sound like a four-year-old bull."

And Andrés, the son, when he heard of his father's plight, appeared as expected and took over his father's contract, because he could not bear the thought of his father dying in the montería or, more likely still, collapsing on the march through the jungle.

Thus, the finquero got the amount of the debt paid in cash by the agent, and on top of it, at the same time he kept Andrés' father and also the growing younger brothers and sisters bound to the finca. Naturally these youngsters would marry and have children in their turn, keeping the finquero provided with new generations of peons.

A finca without permanent labor has no value whatever. The only farm workers a finca can rely upon are the families who belong to the finca as an inseparable part of it.

"Pues, all I can tell you," Celso said when Andrés had finished his tale, "is that you're just as much in the shit as I am."

"You said it, manito, up to our necks. You've got a girl waiting for you and so have I," said Andrés. "Our girls will probably have to wait until their little wells dry and shrivel up and are no longer good for anything."

"Seems, after all, I'm slightly better off than you," Celso stated. "I can run away. They can't take it out on my father, nor do I have any captive brothers whom they could drag off in my place. But in your case they'd get hold of your father and to save him you would again have to leave your girl and your ox carts."

"Well, then, you stupid ass, why don't you run away," Andrés asked, "if neither your father nor anybody else can be dragged off in your place?"

"Stupid ass yourself. Where can I go? If I want my girl I'll have to return home. She wouldn't leave the village. There she has her land and her father and mother and her whole clan. If I return to that pueblecito, the police will get me in three days. Then I'm returned to the monterías, and I get a hundred lashes or perhaps two hundred and I'm one hundred or two hundred pesos deeper in the hole for the expenses of catching me. I'm not that dumb. And if I can't go back to my girl, what's the use of going anywhere else? Wherever you go you have to work, and work damned hard. Nobody gives you a single centavo for nothing. So I might just as well work at the montería. Run away, move freely as you wish, where to? From one place of work to the next. Wages are the same everywhere—coffee plantation, montería, ox carts, mule driving. How many years did you say you been working as a carretero? All right. Can you buy yourself a milpa, even a very small piece of land to grow corn and beans? Nothing. You haven't got a thing. For years and years you've driven carretas and worked harder than all your oxen put together. And now you can't even pay your father's debt. You even had to transfer into the contract the debt you owed the owner of the carretas for whom you slaved. Run away? Where to?—Here, take this cigar. I can roll them better than you. That's something you'll learn in the monterías—how to roll a good cigar."

22

On the first day the troop arrived at a small ranchería, a settlement called Chiquiltic, an Indian name which means "ticklish place." The main building was an adobe hut, located on a rise from where the owners overlooked all the miserable huts of their peons, which were located around the base of the heights.

Some of the troop camped among the huts, while others rested at the edge of the woods and some even inside it.

Although the march on this first day had not been long, the distance covered was, however, considered "una jornada regular," a regular day's journey. A fair-sized river had had to be crossed. That meant a lot of work. The animals were unloaded and their packs carried across the river on the heads of the men. Had the loads remained on the mules' backs they would have been completely soaked, because the water was deep enough to come up to the men's shoulders.

The animals had to be allowed sufficient time to dry out, otherwise they would become saddle galled. Then they were loaded again. All this took time and shortened the marching day. As a result the afternoon was well advanced when the troop arrived at Chiquiltic.

Andrés and Celso squatted at the same fire.

"Go and see," Andrés said, "if you can get ten centavos worth of lard in the main building up there or in one of the huts. Here, take this can along."

Celso left. In every hut he saw men of the troop shopping: eggs, dried meat, lard, tortillas, chile, piloncillos, totopostles, fruit.

When he returned with the lard he said: "What do you think of that, manito? We've got a new one."

"What do you mean, a new one?"

"A new one in the trap. A volunteer, eager to go to the montería. And for pure pleasure, too."

"Don't give me that, burro. Pure pleasure. Crazy."

"But it's true, I tell you. He has been hanging around the place for three days, I was told, waiting for the labor battalion to pass by. So just when I was up there in the main house asking for manteca, the guy approached Don Gabriel. Far as I could see Don Ramón was not about. Perhaps he was off whoring some of the widows somewhere."

"Widows? How do you know?"

"Yes, widows. That's what I said. There're always widows around these rancherías. More widows than married women. Ask me. Well now, Don Gabriel had strung up his hammock for the night up there on the porch of the 'casa grande' where the ranchero lives with his family. Myself, I wouldn't care to sleep there. Infested with fleas, ticks and full of rats. You can't walk without stepping on them, what with all the maize stored up in the house. So that fellow pops in and asks meekly if Don Gabriel might not perhaps need one man more for the monterías."

"And voluntarily? I don't believe it."

"But it's true, mano, I tell you."

"All right, go on. What happened then?"

"So now Don Gabriel examines him from every side and

angle, squeezes his biceps, then his thighs—well, you know how he plays it up with new ones, trying to make it look very important—and then he says in a tone as if he were making the guy a valuable present: 'Bueno,' he says, 'bueno, matter of fact, I'm full. Got more than I need. Anyway, since you're begging me, all right, I'll take you along. One tostón, fifty centavos a day. Wages start with the first full working day. Any debts? No? Good. Cuanto enganche quieres? How much advance? Well, take five pesos enganche, so that you can buy your supplies for the march. We'll make out the contract in the montería. Saves you lots of cash. Need not pay any stamp tax, see? Only my commission. It's fifty pesos. Go down there and find yourself a fire where you can sit with the other muchachos. What's your name? Santiago, eh? Santiago what?"

" 'Santiago—Santiago—' He fumbled around, rummaging in his mind for a new name.

" 'Well,' said Don Gabriel, 'don't you know your own name?'

" 'Por_supuesto que sí, patrón. Santiago—Santiago Vallejo, a sus órdenes.'

" 'Spelled with a B-burro or with a V-vaca?—Forget it. Doesn't matter. Bueno, on your way, Santiago.' Don Gabriel dismissed him with a short gesture and continued swinging in his hammock. You see," added Celso, "the fried turkeys fly straight into his mouth. Someone always even opens Don Gabriel's mouth for him, so he won't have to overwork himself."

"Where is he now, the new one?" asked Andrés.

"Wandering around the chozas, buying his supplies. Look, here he comes."

The new man came straight toward the fire where Andrés and Celso sat, probably because he saw only two at this fire while around most of the others six, eight and even twelve men were squatting.

When he was still about five paces away Andrés shouted: "Hey, you don't mean to tell me that it's Santiago, from Cintalapa!"

"Keep your maldito hocico shut, Andresíto, if you know what's good for you. I told that mangy dog, the enganchador, that I was from Suchiapa, and I warn you, cuate, if you ever tell a living soul that I was a carretero, I'll knock out all your teeth. And," with a gesture at Celso, "that goes for you too, mano. Say, Andrésito, who is this guy sitting here with you anyway?"

"You needn't worry about him. He's all right. Name's Celso. Used to slave at coffee fincas down Soconusco way. Now he's an old hand in caoba. Finest guy in the whole mahogany army. May God damn caoba forever and ever."

"Amen," Celso said.

Santiago began to unpack his net.

"You know," Andrés explained to Celso, "Santiago used to be a carretero together with me, working for the same boss. For years we drove in the same ox cart caravan."

"Suits me. And why shouldn't he?" Celso said indifferently.

"By the holy soul of a working ox, hombre, Santiago," Andrés said with a happy grin, "you're the very last guy I expected to see in a caoba army. But now, to tell the truth, life can't be so utterly miserable any longer with you around. Old comrades meet again. It's really sort of a consolation."

"Well, you know, m'ijo," said Santiago, while putting the beans on the fire, "you know I've always had a deep longing for the monterías. They say that if you've been a carretero for several years you'll get a dispensation from purgatory without paying any goddamned padre for it. But you know it's also said that people who've been in the monterías for two years aren't accepted in hell, because nobody can scare them with boiling chapopote, tongs and pitchforks any more. So I'm asking you, then where is all the fun in hell? I always had a great desire to see how things really look in the monterías. That's why I'm here."

"Aw, hombre, be yourself," Andrés laughed. "Don't give us that. Come across with the real story. Que mosca te cayó en el caldo? Come on."

Santiago made a wry face and said: "Well, manito, the fly in my ointment means ten years in the penitentiary, and if the judge has overeaten the day before or, worse, has a horrible hangover, it might run up to a stretch of twenty years. So now you'll understand my longing for the monterías somewhat better. And you'll also understand why I'd feel forced to beat you up so thoroughly that you won't know which side is which if you tell anybody here or anywhere else a word about it. And that goes for you, too, Celso."

"You can trust us, manito. I vouch for Celso's good behavior," said Andrés.

Santiago stirred the beans, poured some of the ground coffee in the little tin pot, threw in a few lumps of brown sugar and added water almost to the brim. When everything was on the fire just as he wanted it and he only had to wait patiently for the beans to cook, he made himself a cigarette by rolling coarse tobacco in a corn leaf, lit it and said: "Whether I could get off with the minimum, that is, eight years, I doubt very much. The little incident really was in fact a bit thick. It would be ten years at the very least. There's a certain lover boy six feet deep in the ground. You get into a mess like that and you never know how it all happened. All of a sudden he lies there flat on the ground and not a peep out of him. And no ointment and no manzanilla brew will do him any good. So you have to rely on your legs."

"But, manito, see here, that's not the way to tell a juicy story," said Andrés. "If you can't tell it straightforward then for heaven's sake keep your trap shut."

Santiago could not keep his trap shut. Nobody can when

something is eating him up inside. He has to get it off his chest, even if it should mean his life. It is not brains or hands, but the mouth that brings the greatest calamities upon mankind.

"You know my girl, that Sinforosa, I had in Cintalapa?" said Santiago.

"Of course I know her. Who wouldn't?" replied Andrés. "Every child knew that she was your woman. Didn't she have a child by you?"

"A child? Three she had. Two died. I was always sure Sinforosa's mother poisoned them. She could never stomach me, that old slut. She told me hundreds of times right to my face that she'd love to see me under ten feet of earth, together with all my bastards. That would really make her happy, she always said. But the girl loves me, and I love her. She's really a sweet thing. So when I was away again for two months off on the road, there was some fiesta, some great goings-on in Cintalapa. A carnival or inauguration of the new Presidente Municipal or some such celebration. What do I know? Dancing everywhere. And lots of beer and tequila and muscatel and anise. Sinforosa, of course, in the midst of it. Twenty years old, very pretty, and she loves to dance. Now, if once in a while she has her little private fun—well, it's just one of those things and I don't begrudge it. A bottle must feel the cork now and then, otherwise it will forget that it is a bottle and out of spite may turn into an ordinary open drinking glass. And a plant must be watered frequently or it withers away. Of course there must be a limit to everything, that's what I say.

"But now, what really got me mad when I heard about it was that such a dirty mug of a peddler should've dared to make her, Sinforosa I mean, and keep her for good. That was too much.

"You know she operates a little store in Cintalapa where she sells all sorts of useful things like thread, needles, safety pins, ribbons, cigarettes, matches, writing paper, pencils, ink, candles which she makes herself to earn more, bananas, mangos, lemonades, well, you know all the stuff people need every day. I bought her that little store with an advance I borrowed from the boss so that while I'm away on the road with the carretas she'd be kind of independent and have something to do and to live off of. Everything was fine and perfectly settled as it should be, if you know what I mean.

"So now, one fine day I arrive with my train of carretas at Cintalapa. I get there and see how Sinforosa is doing and everything seems just like always.

"So Sunday comes. I went to the poolroom where all the town yokels used to gather. One of them was well up in his cups. He grinned and yelled: 'Hello, amiguito Santiago, how do you like being a second-hand stopper?' 'Shut up,' hollered a few of the other guys hanging around, and one of them says to me: 'Don't listen to him. He's stinking drunk. He doesn't know what he's babbling about. Since yesterday he's been so full of booze that it's running out of his ears.'

" 'Well, what exactly do you mean?' I asked him, dragging him by his shirt collar until he got bluish all over. He could only squeak: 'Just ask your chicken, she can tell you better than I.'

"I pushed him over the pool table and rushed off. 'Now you'd better come across with the whole damn story,' I said to her. 'I know how things stand. So you might just as well tell me the rest of it.' Since Sinforosa believed the boys had told me everything up to the last little detail, she broke down and really talked about herself and this guy.

"He also owned a store. In a small town like Cintalapa, you know, everyone knows everybody else. So at the public fiesta he pumped her up to the brim with muscatel. You know that goes down like honey with cream, then suddenly you don't know your own name any longer. He took her to his house so that her mother shouldn't see her so drunk, that's what he explained to her. His wife was not at home. But you see, Sinforosa didn't know it. Otherwise she wouldn't have gone to the house, that's what she told me honestly. After they had been alone in the house for some time he started trying to make her. She pushed him off and wanted to leave and go home. But he struck her with a bottle over the head, made her lose her good sense and threw her on the bed.

"Worst thing is, after that she gets seriously entangled with the peddler. May hell get him! Every time I think of it I just could jump out of my own skin and hang it on the washline.

"Bueno, manitos, you know how women are built. Always itching for something. Talking sugar to you all the time, but the fact remains that you never know where you actually stand with them. You never know what is the truth and what is a blazing lie, where it begins and where it ends. And so she ended up that it hadn't been her fault at all, that she had been miserably seduced by that brute and hit by him several times over the head, and that's why she didn't know how it all happened. But then when she finally admitted she had been with that sonofabitch uncountable times, she said she had to be with him because he had sworn in her presence, por la Santísima, that he would stab her in cold blood, and that he would stab his wife and his children also to make the job complete, if she wouldn't consent. 'What else was there for me to do?' she finished up her story.

" 'You could've said No and No and forever No,' I told her, 'and just because you didn't say No it is now my turn to tell you how to behave when I'm on the road.'

"So I took off my belt and let her have it. I had to do something at least to make her realize how matters stood. And when she had gotten what she honest to God deserved, she whined: 'Santiago, mi cielo, mi vida, mi alma, my life and my very soul, you know that you and only you mean everything to me por toda la eternidad, forever and ever.' Sounded fine and elegant, like you hear it at the tent show. I believed her. And because I believed her, I was off the next minute, straight to that peddler. 'Hey, tu, cabrón, you goddamned stinking worm, what've you done to my woman?' 'I?' says he, grinning. 'Me? What have I done to her? She placed herself very conveniently—or didn't she? How otherwise could I have made her? Get out of here, you loafer, you good-for-nothing, you drunken tramp, or, by God Almighty, I'll call the police and have you thrown in the calabozo till the rats leave nothing of your carcass but the naked bones.'

"He reached back for the gun he carried in the holster on his belt. In front of me, on the counter there stood a bottle of tequila, more than half full. So I grabbed the bottle and hit him over the head. He pulled at his gun but it had caught on some button of his pants. I pushed him against the wall and continued clubbing him with the bottle. And since I was at it I went wild. I kept on beating him until the bottle broke over his head and all the tequila ran over him. Then I caught a wooden board that was nearby and kept on hammering him. I wanted to beat the stuffing out of him so he wouldn't think of Sinforosa for weeks. He was bleeding heavily and I thought that by now he must have had enough. So I went on my way.

"I hurried to Sinforosa and sat down to have something to eat. I told her that, for a while at least, she wouldn't be bothered by him. 'But what have you done?' she asked, frightened and getting pale all over. 'I just pasted him a few on the noodle same as he did to you, to pay him for service rendered.' She began to cry and sob: 'The poor, poor man. He hasn't done a thing, not a single thing, it was all my fault. You're a dirty beast. I don't want to have anything more to do with you.'

"While I was thinking, trying to realize how matters really stood, Pedro, the head man of the caravan, came and told me: 'Hey, Santiago, run for all you're worth! The police are after you. They're looking for you in the poolrooms. They'll be here any moment. Don Manuel, whom you beat up, is dead.' And hearing this, Sinforosa, like a mad savage, shouted: 'Dead? You murderer! You've killed him, you murderer!' And she ran to the door and out into the middle of the street and yelled with all the power she could muster: 'Policía, aquí, acá, aquí está el asesino, here is the killer, he is right here! Come get him and shoot him like a mad dog!'

"So I grabbed my hat and bolted out of the house. I ran along back of houses toward the wide open space on the outskirts of the town where we had made our camp. 'Quick, quick, I've got to leave, because the police are after me,' I hastily said to the muchachos who were there, fixing the carretas. I ran to my carreta. I grabbed my pack and when I was ready to leave, Pedro came. He gave me four pesos and told me: 'Here, take this money and get a good start. We'll tell them you haven't been here so they'll look for you all over town for another two days. Muy buena suerte, lots of luck. I'll go and look up your girl and paste her a few good ones straight in the face. Thank all the saints that you're rid of that one.'

"I went off across the fields and through the bushes into the thicket, avoiding every village where there were police. And here I am. Nobody will look for me in the monterías. They wouldn't think of it. In two, three, four years the whole thing will have blown over. If I outlive the montería, and why not, the Republic is so big and wide that I won't lack a place to sit down where nobody will bother me."

23

After half a day's march in the jungle the troop arrived at a lake. The lake was small but beautiful and romantic in its quietness. The agents blew their whistles, signaling a halt. All the men got down on their knees and dropped their packs. Then they went down the steep bank, washed their hands, rinsed their mouths, filled their jícaras with water and prepared their pozol.

Celso, Andrés and Santiago had been marching together, one behind the other. Since the camp near the finca La Condesa, Paulino had joined the three. Paulino was considered a sort of philosopher by everyone, because he had piled up a vast experience in the art of catching little black kittens.

It was only natural that these four young men should have joined each other. They stood at about the same level of inborn intelligence. Andrés, the former ox-cart driver, possessed the best education, which he had absorbed through his own efforts and inclination. The other three had probably lacked the opportunity as well as sufficient personal ambition.

Andrés was the quietest, the most serious and the most peaceful of the four. Celso, Santiago and Paulino relied more on their fists and on rapid action than on long meditation and careful consideration. Andrés was the strategist, the other three were tacticians. Andrés was inclined to take life seriously and thus make it harder for himself. The other three took life in their stride and adapted themselves until they believed that they had made their situation tolerable, even somewhat easier. The four of them, just like the rest of the troop, had fallen under powers which were stronger than they were and over which they had no influence whatever. But every power rests upon recognition. No power can exist of its own and continue like a constantly renewed universe. No dictator is so strong that his power cannot be evaded. No dictator can give orders where the will to obey him does not exist. Concentration camps, Siberia, slave labor, tortures and death penalties have their narrow limits, because the will to non-obedience, to resist brute force, is, in the end, infinitely stronger than the will to attack or to exercise a similar brute force.

The power which determined the fate of these four muchachos was invisible and intangible. It was impossible for them to comprehend that their fate was determined not by the agents or the contratistas of the monterías but by the dictator, whose actions, in turn, were influenced by the idea that the welfare of the Republic was guaranteed only if native and foreign capital was granted unlimited freedom and if the peon had no other object in this world than to obey and to believe that which he was ordered to believe by the authorities of the State and Church. Anyone who had other ideas concerning human rights was whipped or otherwise tortured until he changed his opinion, or was, with the blessing of the Church, shot if he spread such ideas.

Even the most intelligent among the muchachos were incapable of seeing clearly where the real power was located and who it was who held it firmly in his hands and therefore could freely dispose of their lives. Everyone in the long chain of men who were interested in the mahogany business was, himself, only a link completely innocent of the cruelties, the misery and the sufferings of the caoba workers. Every one of them, had he been asked, would have replied: "I never knew that anything like that could happen. I'm very sorry and I'll see if anything can be done about it."

Occasionally, the cries of pain of the men tormented in the jungle reached the dictator's ear. Then he got very mad, officially mad, and ordered a commission to investigate. But then more important matters were placed on his desk and he forgot to find out whether the investigating commission had really started an investigation, or whether his order to send an investigating commission had only served for a dozen of his partisans, always after a lucrative sinecure, to get a high per diem for ninety days, without even spending a single night outside the city to find out whether those cries of desperation had actually sounded or if they were but some deceptive illusion or poisonous propaganda of the ever-increasing movement against the dictatorship.

The workers in the monterías, even had they discovered where that power which had such terrible influence on their fate was located, would have been unable to eliminate it or even shake it. This anonymous power was intrinsically interwoven with all other powers in existence. The import-export companies in New York were not sovereign in their might or influence. Their power, in turn, depended upon the good will of the hardwood import companies in London, in Liverpool, in Le Havre, in Hamburg, in Rotterdam, in Genoa, in Barcelona, in Amsterdam and in Copenhagen. And the power of all these companies again depended upon the good will of the thousands of hardwood-consuming companies and individuals which in their ramifications and branches could, in hundreds of instances, be followed to village carpenters in the smallest countries. That fundamental power was so dispersed, so ramified, so branched out and so interlaced with all the activities of human

production and human consumption, that not even God Himself could have pointed a finger at a certain man and said: "This
is the one who is holding the original power which determines
the fate of the mahogany workers."

As impossible as it would have been to explain to the peons
that an office in New York, full of diligent, tireless, typing and
calculating men and women, in constant fear of losing their
jobs, did not determine the fate of the troop which was marching through the jungle, it would have been less possible still to
convince the peons that the fate of a hungry jobless worker is
not determined by a person but by a system. Not even the
ablest of agitators, the most fiery speaker, would have found a
single man in the entire troop to whom he could have explained,
with even very limited success, what is meant by a system.

For all these Indian lumbermen, including the fairly intelligent Andrés, everything that was not linked immediately to a
person or an animal or anything visible, was incomprehensible.
These muchachos recognized as the fateful power governing
them those who were nearest, those whom they could see and
those whose whip lashes they could feel. Strangely enough,
their hate rarely even reached the agent. They excused the
agent by agreeing that it was his business and his mission to
recruit men for the monterías, just as it was the business of
cattle traders to buy cattle for the butchers in the cities. The
men whom they considered as the real brute force and power,
because they exercised their power directly, were the coyotes
for the agents, the capataces and the drivers of the troop.

The national dictator, who perhaps could have altered the
fate of these marchers, was as strange to them and as far beyond
their call for assistance as God in Heaven. Their dictator,
whom they knew and saw, was the capataz. They could reach
the capataz. To implore him to be less cruel never occurred to
them for a moment. But the capataces, who came from the
same blood as the Indian peasant, denied all blood relation and,

even more strongly, all common solidarity. The capataces thought that the more brutally they treated the peons and the more mercilessly they helped their masters to catch new victims, the closer they were socially to the ladinos, the agents and the contratistas.

The peons, to avoid bursting from the fury within them, saw no other recourse but to be in permanent rebellion against the capataces, not only during transports, but even more so in the monterías. Day and night it was their constant thought to get, for once, one of those brutes under their fists. It never occurred to a single one of the peons to eliminate the capataces by a combined attack on the system of which a capataz was but a tool. The greatest extreme to which they might be driven by utter desperation was that of destroying the monterías, just as, a few years later, the revolutionary peons in the state of Morelos destroyed all the sugar factories, razing them to their foundations, because they considered los ingenios, that is, the sugar refineries, the source of all their sufferings. And it was for exactly the same reason that during the revolution the most ferocious attacks of the revolutionaries were against the priests and the churches. Whatever the kind of oppression, it always causes the same consequences, because men never change.

24

At the lake where the troop now rested, the march was delayed for quite a while. Several of the pack animals had met with difficulties in crossing a troublesome brook on the way. The brook, very stony, with numerous deep holes washed out by the stream, had caused several animals to stumble and fall. Besides, broken-down trees obstructed the ford. A new detour had to be opened through the thicket to get the animals across. A large part of the troop had already arrived at the lake, but an equally large part had not yet even crossed the brook. The head of the column had to wait until the rest caught up with it. And of course this rear guard also needed rest after its arrival.

When the vanguard had already advanced two miles and the main troop was just about to start, a messenger from the van arrived to say that a bridge would have to be built across a swampy stretch, because the animals were sinking in the mud. As the path was so narrow that only one animal, horse or mule, could pass at a time, it was decided that the main troop should remain at the lake until further notice. It was also announced that no other general rest period would be allowed during this day until they came to the next campamento, still a good distance away.

Because of the limited width of the trail, only a few men could be employed in the construction of the bridge.

"Well then, we can lay in a good supply of sleep," said Santiago, stretching himself out on the ground.

"I'll do the same," Andrés mumbled.

Celso, however, did not feel sleepy. Too much was on his mind at this moment. He tried to find an answer to the question: Why had fate torn him so mercilessly from his native village, from his girl and from all the things that he needed to carve out a life, rich or poor, that he could call his own?

He did not let anyone know what was inside him, how much he suffered and how sad he felt, so sad, indeed, that at times he believed that his soul was crying, filling his whole being with tears. The character of his race would not allow him to show his feelings.

But at night, when he lay down to sleep, these feelings began to gnaw at him. Then he evoked images of revenge upon those who were responsible for his undeserved fate. In his mind he saw the capataces, the agents and the contratistas die under terrible tortures. He saw them imploring help and himself squatting, looking on their torments as unmercifully as they had been merciless with him. These phantasies excited, enraged, tired and exhausted him more than any sexual phantasy could have done. Afraid of these imaginings and their prostrating consequences, he was always glad to overwork himself during the day so that he would fall asleep the moment he stretched out on his petate.

On the rise where the troop was resting pine trees towered into the sky. Some grew close to the lake. The pines reminded him of his village and of the peaceful little huts in his comarca. The huts were built of adobe, with no windows and no furniture. The fire burned on the close-packed earthen floor in the middle of the hut. When his mother was cooking, the whole hut filled with smoke, which escaped only slowly along the edges of the walls near the palm-thatched roof where the beams left a small open space. But the pinewood smoke drove away scorpions, venomous spiders and mosquitos hiding in the palm roof.

Here the ground where they sat was thickly covered with pine needles, each as long as a finger. It reminded him of the feast days in his village, when the dirt floors of all the huts were thickly strewn with green pine needles, more beautiful than the finest rug, filling the hut with a pungent aroma more agreeable than the costliest perfume.

There he squatted with his arms around his knees, looking at the gigantic pine trees.

"Andrés," he said, "did you also have pine needles in your jacalitos at the finca on festive days?"

"Yes, of course."

Andrés, thinking of his carretas and of who might be driving them, and of how the boys at this moment were possibly stuck in the mud, was deeply moved by the question. He, too, was reminded by this rug of pine needles of his home. And, suddenly, he thought of his girl, Estrellita, his little star, whom he had to leave behind and with whom he had hoped to live some day in a little hut, with pine needles for a rug on the earthen floor.

"Bueno," Celso went on, "if you also have pine needles in your casitas and they remind you of how fine it is at home, you had better take a good, long look at these pines here. Take leave of them. These are the last pine trees you'll see in years. Perhaps they are the last you'll ever see. Because we are Los Perdidos, the lost men. And whether you'll ever return and see pine trees again in your life, not even your patron Saint Andrew could tell you. You'd better take a good noseful of the smell of these gorgeous pines around here with you to the monterías."

Andrés picked up a little twig which lay by his side, played with it, smelled it and, without thinking, stuck it into his pack.

"Great idea," Celso said, watching him. "I'll do the same. To own such a twig and to take it into your hands in the evening at the fire in the montería is like a little piece of hope. Even if it's dry it will always mean hope and you won't forget that, somewhere in the world, there grow pine trees and that, somewhere, somebody is waiting for you, thinking of you, no matter how badly things go with you."

Andrés lost his sleepiness. He sat up and came a little closer to Celso. For a while they did not talk. They only looked down upon the lake, where small ripples glittered in the sun.

"You had better get yourself sufficient pine splinters right here," Celso said. "If you don't collect your 'ocote' here, you won't get any along the whole road, and then you'll have to light a fire with dry shit. Ever tried it? It works, I tell you. It works. But it must be horse or mule shit. That of the capataces is no good. It only stinks like hell, just like the whole goddamn gang. I don't know of anything in this world which I'd do with greater devotion than push my machete through the bowels of two certain coyotes. That would be real pleasure. And to be hung and buried right here for killing those two would be heavenly joy. You know, those two crooks who snatched me in Hucutsin. For five duros. Five lousy pesos. But I tell you, mano, I won't soil my honest machete with their stinking insides."

"I've not the slightest idea what you mean, cuate," Andrés said, without taking his gaze from the lake glittering in the sun.

"Soy algo adivinador, kind of prophet, sonny." Celso grinned maliciously. "Didn't you know that I can foresee exactly what is going to happen to those goddamn bloodsuckers right on this march? I believed you smarter than you are, mano."

"I'm not good at guessing."

"You would be good at guessing if you knew what happened at the last settlement, the one we left only this morning. You see, yesterday I had to help to rebuild the fence where the mules had broken through. I had dug a post into the ground and when the muchachos pulled hard with the vines from the next post, the one I had just stuck in toppled over. Now, I ask you, how can you sink in a post if you can scratch out a hole only with the machete and with your hands, and if that cursed capataz won't wait until you've properly tamped down the soil around the post? The post can't hold, see? So that son-of-a-bitch dealt me one that just doubled me up, I can tell you. Damn it. Half an hour I stay there, picking thorns and stings from my hands because they were boring deeper and deeper in between my fingers. You can't grab the posts properly and work with thorns pricking your hands. It's torture. So along comes the other son-of-a-bitch and he says: 'Hey, you golfo, you stinking vomit of a mule, so you're having yourself a jolly holiday. I'll give you your holiday.'

"And with that he let me have half a dozen with his mule whip. I didn't say a word. Not one word, I tell you. What's the use of quarreling? No words. No arguments. Action. And in the evening I acted. I read the fate of those two coyotes who sold me for five duros and who now want to have their fun with me on this march. But by now I know their destiny as well as my own. I told you, I'm a prophet. Not my fault. It's written in their hands that the bitch who put one of the two into this world won't see him again among her brats. And the other whore who spit out that second reptile also will have one bastard less before we reach the monterías, I can tell you that."

"It's true, they are a pair of stinking bastards," said Andrés, "and if asked I'd say it will be more pleasant at the montería if fate takes good care of them."

"Of that you can be sure, mano. Life will be far more comfortable without those two. The lowest scum on this earth are those who hit the defenseless. And those snatchers, if you meet one of them alone and you happen to have the better of him, they're the dirtiest whining sons of whores you can imagine. Whimpering, trembling and shaking all over worse than an old woman."

"Did you tell those two whip-swingers what you read in their hands?" Andrés asked. "It might not be so bad if you told them all about it so they can be more careful on their way."

Celso looked at Andrés with half-closed eyes. He was not quite sure whether Andrés meant what he said or if he just wanted to be funny.

"Do you really mean," he asked, "that I should warn those two of what fate has in store for them?"

"Well—it is—I mean to say, they're Christians and not heathens," said Andrés hesitatingly.

"Christians, you said? Beasts, that's what they are, but not Christians." Celso said it in a tone as if fate had already taken care of the two capataces. "And let me give you some brotherly advice. If you tell that pair of whoremongers one single word about my prophecies or if you breathe it to anyone else in the troop, I swear you'll be spitting out all your teeth. Keep your goddamned trap shut." He sighed. "Well, there are the cabrones whistling to continue our march. Let's get up."

25

The whole troop came to life once more. The arrieros loaded the pack mules, then tightened the girths. Soon yells and shouts sounded all over the place: "Ora, mula, adelante. Que diablos y cabrones. Pronto Prieto, pronto. Abran. Abran!"

The yells and blasphemous oaths of the arrieros were returned a hundredfold by the echo from the lake.

The capataces and drivers, not to be outdone by the arrieros, hollered at the troop. The whips cracked and the agents blew their whistles furiously, while the men shouted to one another.

After a short march the troop arrived at the newly constructed bridge. The bridge, built rapidly and precariously, crossed a swamp.

The swamp had a width of approximately twenty yards. Obviously nobody had ever cared to find out how far it stretched out to the left and the right. A greenish-black color, it was full of little watery pools and puddles. In the leaden, heavy, dark green enclosure of the jungle, the swamp seemed far blacker, more ghostly and more terrifying than it would have appeared in clear, open sunlight. If someone took a single step into it, putting his foot down hard, he sank immediately

169

up to his knee. The mud stuck to his leg as if it were a live being. It clung firmly and sucked. You had the sensation that somebody was pulling the foot down, slowly but unceasingly. If you brought the other foot close to pull out the first one, the second foot also sank into the ooze and was sucked down. Panting, sweating, breathless, and with your heart on the point of bursting, you managed to reach firm ground where you could sit down, regain your breath and think of what to do next. There is no turning back in such a swamp. It's either ahead or perish.

That had been the experience first of the ancient Mexicans, the Aztecs, and later that of the Spaniards and Frenchmen who came searching the jungles for the legendary holy cities of the Mayas, where walls and roofs were supposed to be of pure gold and where the women wore necklaces with pearls and diamonds as large as ducks' eggs. When these first explorers and adventurers found the cities in ruins, they looked for gold mines and diamond fields. They did not find those, either, and so finally they had to be satisfied with caoba which, if handled wisely, could be transmuted into gold. Thus, their efforts and their expeditions had not been completely in vain.

The caoba caravans were in no way prepared to go exploring for other routes. Their corn rations were calculated so precisely that a delay of two days along the march might be fatal. The animals used by the montería caravans were accustomed to dry, hard plains and mountain passes. One can lead these animals through brooks and across rivers, but not easily through swamps. Neither blows nor kind words nor the most blasphemous oaths can drive them across a swamp once they sense danger.

The danger actually existed that the animals might sink out of sight with their loads, so the old hands among the arrieros did not even attempt to force the passage through the swamp. Experience had taught them that it took less time and offered greater security for both the load and the animals if a bridge was built.

Tree trunks, branches and twigs with heavy foliage were spread over the swamp. When it is covered by heaps of branches with all the leaves left on, the swamp loses its dangerous aspect for the animals. Besides, and this is a very important point, the ground acquires greater firmness. This cover, of course, oscillates and wiggles over its swampy foundation, and that makes the going insecure for the animals. They step cautiously, but at least they advance. At one short section of the swampy terrain a sort of bridge was built of long, stout trunks, held together with bindweed, and well covered with branches and twigs so that the animals' hoofs wouldn't slip between the trunks.

When everything was ready the whistles blew, and the mule drivers took over. The most spirited animals were already pushing on, while the men were still busy piling branches and twigs. These lively animals went so fast that the muchachos had to jump out of their way so they wouldn't be trampled on.

The site echoed with the wild shouting of the arrieros who were incapable of pronouncing a single sentence that was not studded with satanic oaths about whoring cabrones, whoring old women and whoring sons of this and of that.

The yells and oaths, the racket of the excited pushing animals, kicking and biting, stamping and groaning, panting and grunting, the squeaking and rattling of the straps and ropes of the packs, the unexpected fall of an animal and its struggle to get up rapidly so as not to be kicked by the following animals, or be pushed off the bridge, enlivened the scene. The shouting and swearing of the arrieros and muchachos, many of whom stood up to their chests in the swamp, attracted a huge throng of monkeys, called gritones. The gritones, high up in the tops of the trees, made terrific howls and roaring bellows that made the loudest shouts of the swearing arrieros sound like sweet whisperings.

All this confused and irritated the pack mules, and the more the animals became excited, the more the feeble mat of twigs and branches sank in the ooze. The last animals stood in the swamp to their girths and crossed the disintegrating bridge at really great risk.

The main troop of men, which had been kept back to make way for the animals, now approached and wore out the last thin remains of the covering and also the last splinters of the bridge. When about half the troop had reached the opposite bank of the swamp, both the cover and the bridge were no longer visible. The swamp looked more horrifying and impassable than when the caravan had arrived. The soft banks had caved in, and some of the trunks had slid off and now lay lengthwise across the black, muddy, sticky water. The next caravan would have to build a new causeway.

26

It happened on the second day in the jungle. Around noon the troop had made a short halt at a site called La Lagunita. Celso had hurt his foot against a sharp rock. He squatted near the water and rinsed off the blood. The signal was given to continue marching.

Celso bandaged the wounded ball of his foot with a dirty cotton rag torn from his shirt. It was slow work because he wanted to tie the simple bandage as firmly as possible, so that it wouldn't slip and get lost along the road.

It was not on account of the pain that Celso bound his foot so carefully, but because of experience. When working in the coffee plantations at Soconusco County, he had seen a young man cut himself slightly with a machete to which specks of earth had adhered. On the following day the man could neither move his head nor his shoulders, and a few hours later he died. With the bandage, Celso meant to protect the wound against poisonous earth as well as new bumps when marching. There was no physician with the troop and none at the monterías. Everyone had to take care of himself and be his own doctor. He who perished only proved that he had no right to live and proved, furthermore, that he was a scoundrel who cheated the agent or the montería out of an important advance.

173

The troop was already on the march. Celso had not quite finished his bandage when the last men passed him.

Back of that group, El Zorro came on horseback. El Zorro, The Fox, was one of the two coyotes who had framed Celso in Hucutsin to earn five pesos for hooking him. The other of the two was nicknamed El Camarón, The Shrimp.

El Zorro had ridden a few hundred paces back to see whether any muchachos were lagging behind. He had found everything in good shape and now came trotting along. He saw Celso squatting on the trail, still busy fixing his bandage.

"Andale, Chamula, ándale, you stinking old mule," El Zorro shouted. "Andale, ándale, do you want to go to sleep here and dream of fucking women? Up with you, up, up, on your feet. The others are already arriving at the montería."

When Celso did not get up immediately, El Zorro struck him across the face with his whip.

"Just so you won't forget, Chamula," he said, "that I'm a ladino and you a stinking Chamula swine, full of lice."

By now Celso had lifted his pack. He said in a freezing voice, "Those blows were all I needed to make up the account, and by the Holy Mother of God Almighty you'll get your due receipt today, cabrón."

Celso said these words in Tsotsil, his native language, but El Zorro knew "cabrón."

"You'll get that 'cabrón' back with interest, tu hijo de una puta that you are," he yelled. "You just wait until we get to the montería. I'll get commissioned to celebrate 'la fiesta.' Then I'll take you on first, while I still have full strength in my arms, and skin you to your rotten bones. You, and that carretero, that Tseltsal joto. Both of you I'll take on first."

"If you ever get to the montería, you offspring of a dirty five-centavo whore," replied Celso. He was following closely after the horse. El Zorro delivered his speeches turning his head backward, because he wanted to be sure that Celso got every word of it and he also hoped to get some pleasure out of the scared or furious face of the Indian. And this was the reason he paid no attention to the trail. The horse stumbled over a root. Along these lonely paths over plains, through bush, jungle and virgin forest horses develop the habit of listening when their riders talk. They turn their ears around and, sometimes, even turn their head. They do not know whether the talk is for them and whether, in the long speech, there might be a word of command which they would want to obey because, if they didn't obey quickly, they might feel the whip.

El Zorro's horse had been paying attention to the speech because obviously it thought that it might contain an order to stop or trot faster.

El Zorro dug his spurs deep in the flanks of the animal and hit it a tremendous blow with his whip.

The horse reared and at the same time turned to the left.

Mad with pain, it jumped so violently that its forefeet sank into holes and both hind legs flew up into the air. El Zorro catapulted over the head of the animal and fell face deep into a wide mud hole. When he managed to crawl out and get to his feet he got a terrific kick from the frightened animal right in his belly. He dropped back, wheezing and swearing the devil out of hell, and tried to wipe the mud from his face.

The horse attempted to turn around but fell down on its side. After some struggling, pulling and pushing it was able to twist the left foreleg out of the hole, whereupon the right sank in deeper. The horse kicked in all directions and finally came to stand on its four legs, panting and trembling with exertion and excitement but patiently waiting for its rider to mount again.

When Celso first saw the horse's foot sinking into the hole and realized what was going to happen, he let his pack slip off his back and leaped out of the way to avoid being kicked by the animal.

El Zorro, barely able to look out through his mud-covered

eyes, yelled ferociously, "Come here, you Chamula pig. Don't you see that I'm over my ears in this shit? Get me out of it, chusco apestoso. Hey, there, for Christ's sake, don't let that damn caballo run away. Hold it, I say. Get a move on, you stinking fart of a Chamula whore."

He stopped yelling and swearing because the thick mud in his mouth was suffocating him. There he sat on his hams, scratching and rubbing the mud from his eyes, from his hair and out of his mouth, spitting and blowing all the while like an angry seal. Nearly dazed from the hard fall, wild with rage, he smeared all the mud back in his face again, unaware of what he was doing. Now he noticed it, spit it out and shook it off his hands. He tried to get on his feet. But, partly because of the horse's tremendous kick which had landed right on his belly, partly because his foot had become stuck in a liana which held him down firmly, and lastly because he was so furious that he could not think clearly, he simply could not stand up.

"You goddamned stinking Chamula swine," he shrieked. "Will you come here and pull me out of this shit or, by God Almighty, I'll whip you into whining shreds and bare every single bone of yours of the last bit of skin."

"Voy, ya voy," answered Celso, "I'm coming; you don't know how fast I'm coming."

He tied the still trembling horse to a tree. When he was about to pick up the reins which were dragging along the ground, he saw a thick broken-off ebony branch, grabbed it and walked close to El Zorro, who was fumbling for his pocket knife to cut the liana which had caught his leg.

Raising his eyes, he saw Celso approaching with the stick.

"What ya want that club for?" El Zorro asked, forgetting to cut the liana with the knife he had finally produced.

His leg still caught by the tough, thick liana, he tried a half turn and came to rest on his knees, holding both his hands high in front of him, spreading his fingers apart and thus letting the pocket knife drop.

Celso's blow passed right between the two hands exactly where it had been aimed. Celso picked up the pocket knife which had not yet been opened and put it back into El Zorro's pants pocket.

Whether El Zorro was dead or not did not worry Celso. He wanted to cede part of the honor to the horse and let it do the rest.

He squeezed El Zorro's foot into the stirrup and buckled the spur tightly to the foot. He fastened the lead rope to the saddle stock. This done, he pulled the horse back on the trail, struck it a light blow on the behind, and the animal ambled off.

El Zorro's body, with its head on the ground, was being dragged along. As the animal walked, the body of El Zorro slid slowly under the horse and that caused the spur to dig into the horse's flank. So the horse started to trot, dragging the body half under and half behind. As the animal's excitement grew it ran faster and so El Zorro's head hammered against rocks, roots and trees. Whenever the horse slowed its gait, the body slipped under again, the spur dug into the horse's flank, and the horse once more began trotting.

Celso could now leave the horse alone. It would fulfill its duty. He took up his pack and calmly continued on his way. The horse had already advanced so far that he could not see it any more.

Celso knew the road well. He arrived at a spot on the road where a very narrow path, hardly visible, led straight across the mountain.

He gathered all his strength. Like a goat, he pushed himself sideways through the thick, thorny bushes and crawled on hands and knees up the mountain. Several times he thought that he would not be able to make it.

Every moment he felt as if his heart were missing a few beats and would stop altogether. His lungs seemed to be bursting.

Soaked in sweat, panting, his mouth wide open and his nostrils trembling, he reached the top of the mountain.

There he dropped on the ground, slipped off his pack, wiped the salty sweat from his eyelids, which seemed glued together, violently rubbed his neck and throat, his left breast, beating it a few times with his fist, took a few deep, resounding breaths, and then picked up his pack again.

Going down the other side of the mountain, at times he stumbled and rolled down as far as twenty yards. But he picked himself up and advanced in long jumps and strides, intentionally falling, gliding and rolling where he thought he could do so without hurting himself. Hard as all this was, he gained a remarkable advance over the troop.

He arrived on the trail shortly after the vanguard passed. The marching men were coming along, one after the other, at irregular intervals.

He did not step out straight from the thicket into the trail. He approached close and hid himself for a while behind bushes. Then he slipped off his pack and let his pants drop down.

With pants half-dropped he stepped out from behind the bushes and entered the trail. Here he pulled and tucked at his pants, drew them up and rolled in his sash again.

"I've just had a fine and healthy belly opening, damn it," he said laughingly, when the next group approached. Some of the boys threw off their packs to rest for a few minutes, to wipe the sweat from their burning eyes and regain their breath. Celso still panted. But none of the muchachos resting around noticed it. Everyone had enough to worry about with his own fatigue.

Celso dragged his pack out of the bushes, fumbled for a thick cigar, lit it and, slinging his pack over his forehead, said: "Bueno, muchachos, I have to be on my way now. My group is up in front. They must've gained a good stretch by now."

He trotted along while the other boys still remained a few

minutes longer for a rest, talking until the next group arrived and also halted for a while in the shade. From a rift in the steep, rocky wall, a thin stream of cool clear water came forth. It was this spring that caused everyone who passed by to feel the urge for a brief rest and to knead himself a small piece of pozol into his drinking water.

27

 Around four in the afternoon the caravan arrived at the paraje. The stragglers, the lame and the ones who had already caught calentura, arrived around five.

Since El Zorro generally rode after the rear guard to drive on the sluggards nobody missed him.

But then a muchacho came along, breathless from running. Excitedly he approached the fire around which the agents and traders were squatting: "Patroncito, oh patroncito, half a mile back there on the road, the horse of El Zorro got caught in a tree stump, and El Zorro fell off."

"Well, if that rascal falls off his horse I suppose he's old enough to get on again by himself," said Don Ramón.

Nobody took the excited boy seriously. The agents and the traders had more important matters on their mind than El Zorro.

"Whether next year we can again collect so large and good a troop as this one, Don Gabriel, not even any goddamned jefe político could guarantee us, much less el gobernador," said Don Ramón, placing some hot beans on a piece of totopostle. "Our business goes from bad to worse and more miserable every day. And on top of it it's a dog's life. You'll learn that one day, Don

180

Gabriel. Here we sit like savages around the fire, without a roof over our heads, feeding like pigs and not like good faithful Catholics. The wife at home alone in her bed, I hope, and this time not a single whore with the whole troop. It gets worse and worse. Every kind of business. And I can tell you one thing, Don Gabriel, one of these fine days not one sapling of caoba will be left the way they cut it without ever planting one single new tree."

Don Gabriel looked at the business far less pessimistically. Compared with his former enterprises, this seemed like a gold mine to him. During the long march, he had only one thought: how to take the business away from Don Ramón and how it possibly might happen that Don Ramón should meet with a lamentable accident of such a kind that nobody would be present who could swear that Don Ramón did not owe Don Gabriel five thousand pesos which Don Gabriel had loaned Don Ramón when they were buying up peons. In case Don Ramón should not meet with an accident of this sort Don Gabriel's profit in the deal would not even amount to one-third of those five thousand pesos mentioned, and Don Gabriel would have to continue working very hard for several years before being able to conduct the business by himself and exclusively for his own benefit.

"Un accidente! Es horrible!" a voice shouted above the chattering conversation of the muchachos who were cooking their meals. Don Gabriel, who had been ceaselessly thinking about an accident which should befall his business partner, paled when he heard the yell: "A horrible accident!" But he saw Don Ramón squatting calmly before him, eating and talking, and so he came back to reality.

None of the other caballeros around the fire got excited. They waited for more precise news. Perhaps it was nothing but a peon fallen into a gully, or some boy kicked by a mule. The caballeros got up slowly to see what it was all about.

One of the boys was holding El Zorro's horse by the reins. As everybody could clearly see, the reins and straps had caught several times in the brush and stumps along the trail.

"Why, that's El Zorro," said Don Ramón. "What has happened? Didn't he know how to handle a horse? Damn it, he seems the worse for wear. You wouldn't recognize him. Jesus Christ, it might as well be somebody else I never saw before. But those are his pants all right. Also his boots and his dried and shrunken leather leggings. And there's no doubt that's his horse."

The horse was covered with sweat. It trembled and its eyes were wide with fright.

"How did that whoremonger manage to get under his horse like that?" asked Don Albán, one of the traders. "He spoils my appetite. Thanks to Heaven that I brought a few bottles of comiteco along, or I'd dream the whole night of this mess."

El Zorro's clothing was torn completely in rags, as thoroughly torn and ragged as his face. The head was a dirty pulp. There was hardly any flesh left on the skull and only a few tufts of hair. His neck was like a wash rag.

"Cut him loose from the saddle, if you can't get him out of the stirrup," said Don Ramón. "Put him over there, near those bushes. We'll bury him later. Unsaddle the horse once it has cooled off and take it to the brook to drink. Pobre bestia!"

The caballeros went back to their fire. There they ate solemnly and talked about every imaginable thing, but only occasionally of accidents which they had witnessed personally or had heard about.

"Break out that comiteco, Don Albán," said Don Gabriel. "I hope that in these circumstances you won't let us suffer from ghosts."

"Of course not, caballeros. Considering the way conditions have developed, the comiteco is yours as much as mine. Help yourself. And don't be bashful. I've got enough with me. Besides, what we drink I won't have to bother to sell at the montería. Salud, caballeros."

Don Ramón called the boy who did the cooking for him and for Don Gabriel: "Ausencio, call El Camarón over here. I want to talk to him."

"Ahorita, patroncito," the boy replied. Then he shouted: "Camarón! Camarón! Lo llama el patrón!"

Ausencio went in search of The Shrimp and found him with the arrieros. The arrieros were of the same social stratum to which he belonged, the stratum of noncommissioned officers in the army. "Ya voy. I'm coming," El Camarón said and followed the boy.

"El Zorro was your campañero, eh?" asked Don Ramón.

"Compañero? Well, yes, in a way, compañero," said El Camarón. "To tell the truth, I only know him because the two of us are working together for you, patrón."

"But at least you know where he came from?"

"How should I know, jefe?"

"Well, where did you two meet?"

"En el calabozo, en Tuxtla, jefe."

"Fine-feathered fellows." Don Albán laughed. "Come here, Camarón, have a drink."

"Muchas gracias, patrón," said El Camarón, taking a gigantic draught from the bottle offered. He did not know whether they would offer him the bottle a second time, and what's inside your belly nobody can steal from you.

"So—in jail? In Tuxtla, eh?" Don Ramón remarked thoughtfully.

"But I was there completely innocent, jefe, believe me. I can swear it by the Holy Virgin and the Child." While saying that, he crossed himself and kissed his thumb in confirmation of the oath.

"And why was El Zorro in jail?" Don Albán asked.

"Well, patrón—it was just one of those things. You know

how they happen," El Camarón replied with a wide grin on his mouth.

"What sort of thing?" Don Ramón wanted to know.

"Well, El Zorro had a girl, a criada, you know. He maintained that she had let herself be made by a carretero. So naturally he had a short but rather lively discussion with the muchacha. You know how it happens. And when he looked close the muchacha was no longer among the living. And there was a terrible scandal. And then he was put away in the calabozo."

"And why didn't they keep him there in jail?"

"Que vá, jefe! They couldn't keep him there. You know how it is. Nobody had seen whether he had killed the girl or whether a stone from the roof had fallen off and struck her on the head. He didn't have a centavo. So nobody was interested in his staying in jail. And after a few weeks they set him free. No evidence, you know."

"Did they let you go at the same time?"

"No, they let me out long before that. I had done nothing. I was there all innocent. Framed, I should say. Such things happen, you know, jefe!"

"Didn't you work for some time as mozo for Don Eliseo in Tuxtla?" Don Ramón asked.

"Right, jefe, that's true."

"Don Eliseo runs a farmacia in Tuxtla. He is my compadre," Don Ramón explained to the other caballeros.

He turned again toward El Camarón. "Don Eliseo had you put in jail because you stole drugs and patent medicines when you opened the cases, and then sold them to Don Ismael, the Turk merchant who peddled them at village fairs and markets."

"Mentiras, damned brazen lies, jefe. I never touched anything that belonged to my patrón."

"Well, just try to touch anything that belongs to us here, you whoring bastard. We won't have you put in jail. We'll just drill a few leaden beans into your guts," said Don Ramón.

Then he went on: "And you and El Zorro, the two of you, were also for some time in jail in Huixtla. Isn't that true?"

"Whether El Zorro did time in Huixtla, I couldn't tell, jefe. By the Holy Virgin and Saint Joseph, I wouldn't know. But I can assure you I was never in that dirty calabozo where one can't sleep because of the millions of bedbugs."

"No? Then how come Don Gervasio here knows you from Huixtla? Don Gervasio, isn't this the same pimp about whom you told me that story?" asked Don Ramón.

"Precisamente, exactly," replied Don Gervasio, the other trader. "You and El Zorro stole eight fine mules from Don Adelino's finca Peñaflor and then you cleverly changed the brands. That done, you and your joto, El Zorro, tried to sell the mules to Don Federico, of the cafetal La Providencia. But you had bad luck. The former mayordomo of Peñaflor happened to be in Huixtla, where he owns a small ranch, and he saw to it that you two thieves were taken care of. Is it or is it not so, you goddamn son-of-a-bitch?"

"I? I change branding marks? I don't even know how you go about it, jefe. May the poor soul of my deceased grandmother roast in el purgatorio if I ever was in Huixtla; never in my whole life have I ever been in jail in Huixtla or in Motozintla."

"I think we'd better not go into the deeds and adventures of you and your crony, El Zorro, in Motozintla and in Niquivil, because we'd end up hanging you just for your own protection," said Don Matildo, taking part in the conversation. Don Matildo was a small agent who had some fifteen recruited men in the troop.

"There, Camaronsote, have another drink," said Don Albán, offering El Camarón the bottle of comiteco.

El Camarón took another deep draught.

"Gracias, caballeros," he said, wiping his mouth with his red bandanna.

"To poke into your life and that of El Zorro would keep us busy until tomorrow night," said Don Ramón, "and even then I doubt whether we'd reach the end. At least you might tell us where El Zorro was from, so we can notify his mother or his brothers or whatever relations he had if any of them cares at all."

"Now that I come to think of it, he might have been from Pichucalco. He knew lots about cacao. I remember his telling me something like that. But I'm not sure about it."

"Well, in that case," Don Ramón announced after a while, "there's nothing left for us to do but dig him in. How about it, caballeros?"

The gentlemen got up.

Half a dozen firebrands were brought along and an adequate site was found, some hundred paces away from the paraje.

"Disagreeable feeling," said Don Ramón, "to bury someone so close to a camp site. Who knows how often we'll have to camp in this paraje again and perhaps squat on the corpse if someone needs to let his pants down."

Some of the boys dragged the body along by its legs. Others approached to watch. Others scratched a hole with their machetes in the earth. Once the hole was about two feet deep, the soil became too hard to scratch deeper. Don Ramón already had lost his patience, and said, "Throw him in there and be done with it."

When the boys lifted the corpse, he shouted: "Un momento, just a moment. Go through all his pockets. Take off his boots and see if he carries anything inside. Leave that ring on his finger, it's only brass with a piece of glass, anyway."

They found eleven pesos and thirty-seven centavos in his pocket, some cigarette tobacco in a little bag and ordinary white paper which he himself had cut to size, the usual flint lighter and a good, strong pocket knife.

"Seems to me you're the only rightful heir of that rascal, El

Zorro, around here," Don Ramón said to El Camarón, "so you can hang on to all that junk."

"Gracias mil, jefe." And very contentedly El Camarón pocketed the money and the few other things. "With your amiable permission, jefe, I might just as well take the ring also. He won't need it any longer, and the ring is still good. It may perhaps be brass, but the women won't know the difference. They want to believe it's gold." And without waiting for permission, he squatted down to pull off the ring. El Zorro's hands, which had been dragged along the road just like the head, were so torn, so smashed that one look at them would have caused delicate people to vomit or to faint. Since the fingers were swollen, El Camarón could get the ring off only by using a lot of his saliva and by pulling, twisting, twirling and squeezing the dead man's finger mercilessly. No sooner did he get the ring than he shoved it on his own finger as though afraid someone else might claim it. After cleaning it with his shirt sleeve, he let it glitter in the moving reflection of the firebrands.

"Now you can throw that stiff in," Don Ramón told the boys. But right away he added: "Un momento, just a moment, muchachos." And he called out loud: "Caballeros, it's God's eternal truth, he most certainly was a goddamned son-of-a-bitch, a filthy raper of innocent women, a scoundrel of a cattle rustler, a lousy pimp, a reptile, a venomous snake in the grass, a dirty bandit, a pitiless murderer and only God in Heaven knows what else, but after all, he was a human being and a Christian. And even if he's bound for hell, let's say an Ave Maria for his soul."

The caballeros and the peons took off their hats, and all of them began to babble: "Ave Maria, Santa Purísima, Santa Madre del Dios Poderoso, sálvanos, ora pro nobis, Santa Purísima, Santa Maria de Dios, ora pro nobis. Amen."

The prayer over, the caballeros picked up a few crumbs of

earth and threw them on the body. The peons did likewise, not knowing why, but because the caballeros did it and what they did seemed the correct thing to do.

Don Albán pulled a red handkerchief from his pants pocket and spread it over the disfigured part of the skull where once El Zorro's face had been. Then he made the sign of the cross three times over the handkerchief and said: "Ahora, muchachos, cover'm up."

The peons pushed the earth, partly with their feet, partly with their machetes, partly with branches, until it covered the body.

Since the corpse filled the hollow completely, the earth thrown over it formed a little rise. Several of the men ran into the thicket with their firebrands, gathering stones which they spread over the rise. Then they threw branches, twigs and leaves upon the grave, and still more stones on top to prevent the branches from being blown away by the wind.

In spite of all this the corpse was in no way really protected against wild pigs or hungry tigers, which could easily pull it out into the open again.

"Make a little cross and stick it in there," Don Ramón advised.

And Don Albán added: "You boys who brought this hombre here and buried him, come over to our fire and have a drink, or you'll dream of it all night."

Then he turned around to the gentlemen. "I think we had better have another bottle for ourselves, caballeros. I think we've earned it. Goddamn it again, by Holy Nicholas, caracoles y carambolas, I never saw anyone in my whole life so torn to rags. Hell, I'm going to take a good hefty gargle of comiteco to forget the sight. Bueno, así es la vida, such is life. Yesterday a happy whoremonger and today torn to pieces and not even safe from being eaten by wild pigs. Santísima Madre de Dios, grant me a Christian death." He crossed himself devoutly several times and then kissed his thumb to make sure.

The gentlemen returned to their fire and prepared for a dreamless night with the aid of still another bottle of "comiteco añejo."

28

 Around the fires of the recruited men the incident
formed the night's topic, not only as the most recent
event, but because it was of such a nature that none would
forget it.

The muchachos who had assisted in the burial got their bottle
of ordinary aguardiente from Don Albán. They felt quite
satisfied with it because they were more accustomed to raw
liquor than to the añejo which the caballeros drank, and which
would not have burned their throats sufficiently to be considered a well-earned compensation for the disagreeable work of
this evening.

Don Albán, to whom the life and death of El Zorro was a
matter of complete indifference, voluntarily took charge of the
burial expenses. When it was all over, he found that El Zorro's
accident had cost him two bottles of ordinary aguardiente and
four bottles of comiteco añejo. One bottle had not been sufficient for the men. He had to sacrifice a second one because,
after a while, some other muchachos appeared who claimed
that they also had had to handle the corpse and that during the
next weeks they would be unable to eat a single bite unless they
could wash down the stink with a good, deep draught.

At the fire where Celso, Andrés, Paulino and Santiago squatted cooking their evening meal, there were a few other boys who had joined the four during the march that day.

None of this group paid the slightest attention to the accident. They only got up for a moment when the horse arrived in camp. After a few cursory looks they returned to their fire.

Celso told them: "Keep out of the way. Means extra work. Don't let yourself be seen around there. No overtime's ever paid in these outfits. Get that straight, cuates."

Following this clever advice none of them attended the burial.

Celso took his pots and pans down to the river to wash.

This done he rinsed his mouth and polished his teeth with his index finger.

Andrés had followed him with his pots and pans.

When both of them squatted side by side on the bank and Andrés saw that nobody was nearby, he said: "How did you know that El Zorro was going to be dragged to death by his horse?"

"Who said I knew? I didn't know a thing," Celso replied calmly. "I only read in the stars that he would kick off. In what way that stinking dog would end, the stars didn't tell me. Nor did his hands. Fact is, I don't bother about such little details. You know my story, don't you?"

"Yes, of course I do. It was related to me when you tried to kill me without even knowing me," Andrés said, grinning.

"You would've done the same, mad as I was when I realized that I had been framed by those two bastards. On that day when I believed you to be a capataz."

"I might have."

"And I can tell you right now, that other whoring bastard won't reach the montería either. Perhaps the other cabrón que chi- su madre, won't even be buried with an Ave Maria. He most probably will be eaten by buzzards and wild pigs. I can't do anything about it. It is just his fate. It's written in the stars. See?"

Andrés laughed. "Well, fate sometimes makes remarkable mistakes?"

"What do you mean?" Celso asked suspiciously.

"When El Zorro's horse arrived here at the paraje, you paid no attention. But I took a close look. Just because you had predicted everything so precisely, I was curious to see how fate worked. And now see here: when a rope opens in a loop and the loop falls around the neck of a horse, let's say owing to some clumsy move, the loop slowly opens more and more until, finally, it drags for its entire length after the horse."

"Perhaps. And perhaps not," Celso said quietly, rinsing his mouth.

"But this rope, as I noticed, could not come loose. The loop had been tied so fast at the noose that the horse could have run a full day and the saddle would never have slipped off."

"Well observed, manito. You're more intelligent than I thought. But a rope can get tightened by itself if the loop gets warped and if it hasn't been coiled properly from the beginning."

Andrés scrubbed a little pot, in which he had cooked his frijoles, with sand. "Right," he said. "Fate acts in such a way that a rope or the harness traces of a carreta get into such a queer knot that it has to be cut. And it does it all of its own. But," and now Andrés grinned widely, "I'd like to know the kind of fate that makes an experienced horseman like El Zorro get his left foot into the right stirrup. How El Zorro must have straddled his horse to squeeze his left foot into the right stirrup no fate can clear up for me."

"Lagarto, lagarto," said Celso. "Damn it all, now that I come to think of it, I almost believe you're right, manito."

"Of course I'm right. I was prepared for fate so I did not get excited, and therefore, I saw many things the others did not see."

"Are you sure nobody else noticed it?"

"Not even Don Ramón. And I'll tell you why. The saddle was almost completely under the horse's belly. In that position of the saddle it looked, of course, as if the right foot was in the right stirrup. All those standing around only looked at the smashed and torn skull of El Zorro, because it was gruesome and interesting. And besides, they cut that cabrón free so fast from the stirrup that nobody had time to think what foot was hanging from which stirrup."

Celso laughed and said: "Well observed and well judged. But I'm not as easily caught as all that, hermanito. Not by you. Not by any agent. And much less by any damned chief of police."

"But I'm not talking of you, cuate."

"Whether you're talking about me or about fate or about hell, is muck and fuck to me. At the paraje La Lagunita El Zorro was still alive and in charge of the rear, as you know."

"All right, all right! Granted El Zorro always had the rear guard under him. So what?"

"Did I march with the rear guard?"

"Let me think. No, that's right. You were not with the rear guard."

"Right, sonny. Right. Correctly observed. All along the whole march I was with the boys from Cahancú, far in front of the main group, practically in the middle, where the mules marched. Just ask any of the muchachos from Cahancú and they'll tell you it's God's truth. So what have I got to do with that stinking corpse if I wasn't with the rear guard and was marching along with the first group of the troop?"

For a while Andrés was quiet. Then he said: "Well, I'll be a goddamned cabrón. I can't make heads or tails out of all this.

I've been thinking in all seriousness that you helped fate along with a little push."

"I? But Andrés, how can you say something like that? I? That miserable coyote? There you missed the mark by a mile. I wouldn't hesitate to tell you, compa, because I trust you. But I can't claim any praise for what I didn't do."

"Well then, I'd like to know who did get even with that pest."

"Who? You want to know? Here in this troop there are a hundred and fifty or two hundred, all forced to march to the montería. Ask any of those two hundred if he would not have joyfully cut El Zorro's throat with his machete if he had a chance to do so without the risk of being discovered. Every one of the whole bunch would have done it. And so would I and so would you. So it's up to you to guess which of them was the jackass stupid enongh to squeeze the left foot into the right stirrup. If you think I'm that dumb, that I don't know which stirrup the left foot belongs in, then you're just as dumb as the guy who did it. Perhaps one of those young sheep from a small godforsaken little village, one of those stupid Inditos who don't even know which end of a horse has the tail and which the ears. But not an old experienced coffee finca hand like good ol' Celso. I know which foot goes in the right stirrup and how to coil a rope properly so that it won't tie in a knot at the noose all by itself. And since none of all this nonsense concerns me, sonny, I am going to lie right now on my petate and get me some good, sound sleep. I don't need any drop of aguardiente to keep me from dreaming of ghosts who have lost their faces."

"You're right, Celso. I'm tired, too," said Andrés.

While the two strolled back to their fire, Celso said: "When I worked on that coffee finca, one day they celebrated the saint's day of the finquero. So el cura comes to hold service. And since I had hurt my foot with a machete, I could not work that day. So I stay outside, right near the door of the little church, where all the ladinos are listening to the prattle. And I just happen to hear el cura say: 'De todos modos, hijos míos, la mejor almohada es una consciencia limpia,' by which he meant to say, 'there is no softer pillow than a clean conscience.' I'll remember that always because el cura put it so well. And so tonight, see, manito, I'll sleep like an angel in Heaven because I've got a pure, clean conscience. And once we get to the Santa Clara Lake, I'll have a much better and much cleaner conscience still. Buenas noches, manito."

29

 The march on the following day was as monotonous as the previous days had been since they left the last settlement.

El Camarón was in charge of the rear. His crony's accident had had a very serious effect upon him. He hardly slept during the night. Over and over again he found himself pondering El Zorro's fate. All morning he had been uneasy. Something he could not define was nagging him. During the march he started wondering how it could have been possible that an old hand like El Zorro could fall off his horse. And even if he had fallen off, how had it been possible that he could not hold back the horse and free himself from the stirrup? The only explanation he could arrive at was that El Zorro had struck his head on a rock, become unconscious, and before regaining consciousness had been bruised and beaten so hard that he died.

Scared as he was, El Camarón had been unwilling to take charge of the rear guard. He preferred the safe center.

But Don Gabriel knew how to tackle him. "Oye, maldito cobarde, you goddamned coward, we're not taking you along just for your health, you wretched bastard. I see you've already got your pants full of shit. What do I care? Back home and

196

hide behind old women's skirts. Good for nothing! We can manage without you. No room in this here outfit for sissies and less so for cowards. Home you go. And right now. You heard me! Off with you!"

To have to march back alone from the middle of the jungle was far worse than to take charge of the rear. So The Shrimp obeyed orders.

He tried to be friendly with the stragglers and keep them close by his side. At the same time he tried to be near the troop so the blow of his whistle could be heard.

However, the peons, agile as cats, and from childhood on accustomed to march and wander over similar ground, took short cuts wherever feasible. In spite of their heavy packs they slid down rocks, jumped lightly over swampy stretches and climbed over gigantic fallen trees. El Camarón, on horseback, had to follow the entire length of the trail. There were periods when he found himself completely alone on the trail. It was then that he felt afraid.

He moderated his harshness against the peons to such a degree that he appeared ridiculous to himself. He tried keeping the stragglers close to him by every imaginable trick. The peons, though, were not deceived. They realized that El Camarón had lost his grip on himself. They also knew very well that El Camarón, however amiable he was for the moment, would make up for it once they had reached the montería. As soon as they saw a short cut they took it and disappeared over the rocks.

This made El Camarón feel all the more uneasy and increased his fear. By now he had become absolutely convinced that someone in the troop had helped El Zorro to meet his end.

Celso was the one El Camarón suspected least of all the men. Celso gave him the impression of an Indian who was mentally lazy and who did his work like an ox, satisfied when he did not fall behind his daily quota.

Celso was not the only man in the troop whom he and El Zorro had hooked for the agents who paid them. There were several, now that he came to think of it, who seemed vengeful and therefore dangerous. Among them, Andrés. The thought got hold of El Camarón that he must guard himself especially against Andrés. Andrés was intelligent and at times openly defiant, given to arguing and backtalk. Worse still, he did not go to the montería on his own and for his personal debts, but in replacement for his old father. So, more than anyone else in the troop, he had reason to be in a vindictive mood.

Around one o'clock in the afternoon, the troop arrived at the Santo Domingo River.

Camp was pitched on the opposite bank after the difficult river was forded.

30

Andrés, enjoying a self-rolled cigar, was sitting on the trunk of a fallen tree a fair distance away from the camp site. He heard a noise. He turned around, gazed at the thicket and thought he saw Celso dart like a shadow from one clearing to the next. The dimness would not allow a clear view but he felt convinced that it was Celso apparently stalking a deer.

He now looked in the direction taken by Celso and noticed, ahead of Celso, El Camarón who, with his hands on his belt, was obviously trying to find an adequate site to attend to some personal business where thorny shrubs would not annoy him too much.

El Camarón was wholly unaware that someone was pursuing him.

Andrés got up and returned to the camp, tending his fire and heating some coffee.

Night closed in rapidly.

After ten minutes or so Celso arrived quietly, sat down close to Andrés, and put his beans and his coffee in the embers.

"Strange," said Andrés. "I haven't seen El Camarón during the whole day."

199

"Are you so deeply in love with him that you can't live without seeing that viper?" Celso asked in a very cool voice. "He's now in charge of the rear and you and I march in the first column of the troop. What do you care about that whoring bastard? To hell with him."

Squatting at the same fire, Paulino grumbled: "Now listen, you boys. Once we're in the montería you'll learn damned soon why we should care about him. I tell you if only I had the guts I'd kill that cabrón just like a louse. That's what I'd do, por la Purísima! But the trouble is I'm too much of a coward."

"Forget it. But what would you think if by a dumb accident, I say accident, he disappeared into the Santa Clara Lake?" Celso squinted his eyes as he said that. It was not clear whether he did so intentionally or whether the smoke coming from the fire bit into his eyes.

"And how is he to fall into the lake?" Paulino asked, grinning all over his face.

"Hey, you, Andrés," Santiago broke in, "if we were here with our carretas he wouldn't last very long. Or would he?"

"As far as I'm concerned," said Andrés, "do what you like. Let him live. Just give him enough rope and most surely one day he'll hang himself."

"That's what I think," said Celso. "Let him live. And about that hanging, it isn't such a crazy idea as one might think. He has his pants full because he's afraid. He runs about talking nonsense, saying that El Zorro is after him, because he took his money and his ring. Pants full of shit, that's what he has."

"Por todos los diablos, who took my salt?" yelled Paulino.

"Don't kick up a row about a few grains of salt," said Santiago. "Here is your damned salt. Stuff yourself with it and I hope you choke."

"About half an hour ago I saw El Camarón disappearing into the bushes," said Celso. "Perhaps he was already looking for a tree to hang himself. But by my opinion his pants were too full to do it by himself. Somebody must help him along, so the rope won't break off. And once he hangs he'll go to hell like oiled lightning, and there he'll be greeted by El Zorro who's going to tell him a few things on account of the money and also on account of that diamond ring."

"Was no diamond ring," said Santiago.

"Sure it was a diamond ring," Paulino insisted. "You're just the one to tell me that I don't know about diamonds. I've had more diamonds in my bare hands than you can count up to. When did you ever see a diamond in all your life? You tell me. Perhaps on your oxen, goats and sheep. Don't make me laugh."

"Now don't be fighting over diamonds we don't have," said Andrés. "What business is it of ours whether it was a diamond or I don't know what."

"Andrés is right, it was no diamond," said Santiago. "It's a blue topaz."

"It's nothing but a piece of common, ordinary glass, and the ring isn't gold either," said another of the boys, Otilio, who was also squatting at the fire and who rarely took part in the conversation of the four.

"You, of course, know everything very well," said Santiago, sarcastically. "And I happen to know that the ring is genuine and worth no less than one hundred pesos. Of course the whoring bastard didn't buy the ring. Up there, near Copainala, he assaulted and killed a Spanish trader and buried him right on the spot and took the ring and all his money."

"Hey, you, Paulino, go and fetch some fuel, the fire is going out," shouted Celso. "These goddamned beans won't get cooked today, and before morning, en la madrugada, I won't get a bite. One can starve here and not a soul in the world gives a damn. Up with you, mozo, get us some wood."

"You get your own wood," said Paulino. "And besides I'm not your mozo."

"Get a move on or I'll paste you one on the trap," said Celso, wielding a stick.

"Paste me one on the trap, you and who else?" Paulino shouted furiously.

"All right, you remain sitting on your stinking hams, Paulinito," Andrés intervened. "I'll go and fetch the wood. Because it won't come by itself. And since Celso cooks our grub we can't expect him to fetch the wood, too."

"Well, let's go together," said Paulino, now calm. "Why shouldn't I fetch the wood? But that guy over there isn't going to order me around. He's as much a damn son of a street whore as I am myself."

It was a long evening for the boys. Once they had started to chatter there seemed to be no end to it during the whole night and nobody got much sleep.

In the early morning, when it was still pitch dark, all the fires burned brightly to boil coffee and heat beans left over from supper. These were mixed with totopostles and chile to get something solid into the stomach at the beginning of the day.

Breakfast out of the way, Celso, Andrés, Paulino, Santiago and some others began getting their packs ready.

Paulino covered the fire with earth and picked up the pine splinters which had not been used up completely. He pushed the charred sticks into his pack.

The muchachos squatted around and took the last draught of coffee from their little tin cans, which once emptied were placed on top of the pack or pushed into the opening of the net.

Suddenly the voice of Don Gabriel was heard: "Hey, you, Camarón, you goddamned loafing cabrón that you are, maldito golfo, where are you whoring around? You come right here, I say."

Andrés jerked his body. He looked at Celso, who remained squatting indifferently on the ground, slowly swinging his little tin cup still filled with some coffee, and grunting to himself: "Shit, shat, shot, corruption and goddamn hell!"

It was still dark, but dawn was coming up fast. Everything took on a gray-bluish shimmering tint.

Andrés could see enough of Celso's face. He was astonished at Celso's indifference. Not an eyelash moved in Celso's face.

But now Celso became aware that Andrés was looking at him attentively with a question simmering on his tightly closed lips.

"Hey, you dirty ox-driver, what are you staring at me like that for?" he said, bad-humoredly. "Do you want me to knock out a few of your teeth this early in the morning? I'm in just the right mood for it. I could strangle you or even myself. That's the way I feel, see!"

"Ahorita, jefe," El Camarón's voice came from the thicket. "Just a moment, a second. I'll be along, a sus órdenes, patrón."

"Bueno," shouted Don Gabriel, "we're off. You take the tail as usual, and start counting right here and see that nobody is missing. Make sure of it and don't come later with a sack full of damn excuses."

"Muy bien, jefe," came El Camarón's answer.

Celso looked at Andrés, got up, lifted his pack and said: "Come on, ox-driver. We're in the first column."

After they had marched for a while side by side, Celso opened up: "Just what have you been thinking?" He grinned. "I know 'xactly what you've been thinking. I'm not a prophet and not a reader of the stars for nothing. But you're up the wrong tree. You see, when you or any of the guys think of something, nothing happens. Only when you don't think at all and don't see anything, that's when fate works. Besides, I was watching you closely yesterday, when you saw me flitting about. I was after a tepescuintle. Some fresh meat wouldn't do us any harm. And another thing, manito, we haven't yet come to the Santa Clara Lake. It's still two good days from here. Within two days and deep in the jungle lots of things can happen."

31

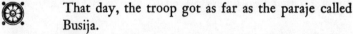 That day, the troop got as far as the paraje called Busija.

The Busija River was wider than the Santo Domingo, but could be forded so easily that it seemed like a Sunday afternoon game. The bottom was stone and coarse gravel. The animals only had to be careful not to stumble over the big stones or to catch their hoofs between them. But since the water was as clear as the air, the horses and mules could see where they stepped.

On the opposite bank there was an ample open space for camping.

It was undoubtedly one of the most beautiful camp sites on the march. But during the night a torrential rain fell, which forced the peons, in the middle of the night, to rapidly build a few emergency roofs. These roofs were not much good, but for a while at least they gave the impression that, without any roofs, the men would have gotten soaked even more. By the first glimmer of dawn, however, they realized that their point of view had been rather optimistic. They could not have been wetter had they spent the entire night sleeping in the river.

On that evening Celso did not leave for a tepescuintle hunt.

He claimed that it was no use wasting energy on it because none of the little animals were in the neighborhood. But like all the others, he went into the jungle in search of sticks, branches, twigs and leaves to build a roof.

As it was the time of the new moon, the evenings were lighter and they seemed more friendly, because the dim light gave the jungle a different tint and made it look less frightening, less threatening after nightfall.

While the boys were squatting around, busy with their evening meal, Celso said: "Close by, there used to be a montería. Now it's dead. It did not have much breath anyway. Of course it was not a real, fully grown montería. It was the kind of montería that you give children to play with, so they won't cry."

Andrés looked around. "But one doesn't see anything of a montería."

Paulino laughed. "There one can see that you're green. You never see much of a montería. You can be in the middle of one and you don't even know it."

"And I don't even see any caoba around," Santiago said.

"As there used, I repeat used, to be a montería around here, how the hell do you expect to see a caoba tree?" replied Celso. "All the mahogany trees have been cut, and that's the reason you don't see them any more. The companies get all their concessions under the condition that for each caoba felled, they have to plant three new caoba seedlings as replacements. They're obliged to do that by their contract or the concession is taken away from them, and on top of that they have to pay a heavy fine. Do you see any young mahogany trees around here? Count them. Not a single one! The companies cut everything and when there is not a single dry stick of caoba left they go on their way. That's what they do."

"During the whole goddamn march I've heard talk of nothing but caoba—caoba morning, caoba noon, caoba night. Caoba and nothing but caoba!" said Andrés. "And by now I'd really like to see real, genuine caoba with my own eyes."

"You should have kept your eyes open, brother," said Paulino. "In the last settlement, all the doors of the huts, all the benches, all the crude chairs which you saw were of pure, heavy caoba. You've got to look around in this world if you want to learn something."

"I could go in search of a good tree for you here," said Celso. "Back in there a few skinny saplings might still be left. But you'll see enough. You'll see so damned many that you'll be spitting blood front and rear and from every hole and gill when you hear the shouting: 'A donde quedó hoy tu jornal, cabrón? Where is your day's quota, you whoring bastard?' Now don't be in such a hurry. The caoba is not going to run away from you."

Paulino who, like Celso, also was an experienced lumberjack, said: "Right beyond the Santa Clara Lake, the vast caoba empire begins. Here where we are now is just a little left-over morsel. Old, experienced hands, like us two, wouldn't think of grabbing a machete, much less an ax. What about it, Celso?"

"Quite right. But I guess we'll have to grab our machetes to build us a casita. The sky looks so dark I'm sure it'll be a cloud-burst of six hours at least. That tiny sickle of a moon we had is already completely wrapped up. Anyway, I figure I'll get down on my petate and wait until it really breaks loose. If the wind turns we may remain dry."

"Tomorrow night we'll be at the Santa Clara Lake," said Paulino. "There it generally rains quite heavily most of the time."

"But sometimes it can be very beautiful around there. Wonderful clear nights." While saying that Celso rolled himself into his serape to sleep.

Before dawn the rain ceased. But heavy clouds were being driven by a strong wind across the sky and it was so dark that it took the arrieros twice the usual time to get the animals loaded in spite of most of the fires being fully ablaze and a few cheap kerosene lanterns lighted.

The packs with merchandise were safely wrapped in petates made of tough coarse fiber and they did not easily let water seep through. But these packs had been lying in deep mud all night. Ropes and girths were wet and could not be tightened smoothly. On the march, once the sun came out, the fastenings would change, the packs would slip down, and they would have to be put back into place and tightened again. Valuable time would be lost and the next paraje might not be reached on schedule.

Celso sipped his hot coffee and stirred his beans in the pan. The others squatting at the fire were busy wringing out their pants and their blankets, then holding them against the fire to dry them. Close to the fire there stood cans, pots and cups in which breakfast was being prepared.

From the island where the caballeros camped Don Gabriel's voice was heard: "Aah-hooooo-ahoo! Camarón! Be damned, where are you whoring around this time? Come here and fast, you miserable worm. Hey, Camarón! Camarooooon! Come here, I say!"

"El Camarón went in search of his caballito, patroncito," said one of the boys, roasting rice for the gentlemen in a frying pan.

"That's right, jefecito," another boy shouted. "Almost every morning El Camarón has to go after his horse. His horse never sticks close to camp. It won't."

"Well, if the goddamn scum can't train it properly, why doesn't he fetter or hobble it?" Don Gabriel grumbled, while at the same time he washed his hands and cleaned his eyes.

Half an hour later Don Gabriel shouted again, this time getting really wild. "By all the devils in hell, donde está este golfo apestoso?—Hey you, Chicharrón," he called one of the boys who was close. "On your way, hurry, go look for that son of a whore and don't dare come back and tell me you couldn't find him."

The slowly reddening sky announced the reborn sun.

The caravan was ready to march.

"What do you want El Camarón for?" asked Don Ramón. "He'll be limping after us. He damn well knows that he's in charge of the rear. Don't worry, a rascal like that won't get lost. And that's really a pity. He hasn't done anything to me but every time he shows up my stomach turns just seeing that bastard."

"I'm not worried about him, not a bit, to hell with him," said Don Gabriel. "But he has the marching list for counting."

Don Ramón had no taste for unnecessary excitement. So he suggested: "Well, Don Gabriel, then you'd better take the rear and count them as best as you can. I don't think any of the men will be missing. Those who have come along this far won't run away now. The road back is too long now and their rations are nearly gone. Let's move on, I say."

"Bueno," replied Don Gabriel. "Entonces yo me encargo de la cola. Though I rather prefer to ride in front or in the middle. But, bueno, someone must take charge of the rear guard." Don Ramón signaled with his whistle to start.

While whips were cracking and the arrieros swearing, El Chicharrón, whom Don Gabriel had sent in search of El Camarón, came running as if all the flames of hell were after him. When quite close, he was unable to say a single word. He swallowed and gurgled and pointed with his arm in the direction from which he had come.

"Bueno, por el diablo, will you talk," yelled Don Ramón at him, "or must I help you with the whip?"

"El Camarón is dead, over there, in the thicket by the slope. He is impaled."

"Impaled?" The caballeros exclaimed in unison from where they sat on their horses.

"Yes, impaled," El Chicharrón repeated. "Virgen Purísima, Madre Santísima, help me, ayúdame and save my immortal soul!" He crossed himself violently, kissing his thumb nervously a dozen times.

"Shut up with your whining," said Don Gabriel. "Let's see what happened. You must be crazy. Impaled? Never heard of it in all my miserable life. Vamos, señores. Let's go and have a look."

One of the arrieros shouted: "Perdóneme, jefe, what are we going to do? The mules won't stand here any longer. They're restless. They'll run away. All loaded. We can't unload them again."

"On your way, then. Go ahead with the animals. We'll follow." Don Ramón whistled once more and the troop started on its march.

"Bueno, jefe," said the arriero in charge. "Hasta luego, until later." He dealt the closest animal a whack on the rump, and they quickly moved on to catch up with those already marching far ahead.

Don Albán called to a group of muchachos: "Hey, you, over there! You better come along! There may be some work."

The moment El Chicharrón had arrived, running and shouting, Celso had said calmly to Paulino and Andrés: "Don't get near. Means extra work. Don't push. There'll be plenty of work for all of us later on." With this he hurried to catch up with his group marching immediately back of the first animals.

"But I'd like to see what happened to El Camarón," said Paulino.

"And what business of yours is it to know what happened to that vinegar pisser?" Celso demanded. "Let him go to hell where he belongs. Or does he happen to be your bed fellow?"

"I'd much rather be the devil's great granduncle than that," replied Paulino.

"Then on your way, and whistle yourself a song," said Celso, falling into his regular marching gait. "If that slotsucker has kicked off, so much the better for you. It means one whip less."

They fell in with their marching group.

Meanwhile the caballeros dismounted and El Chicharrón led them some three hundred yards deep into the thicket.

They found El Camarón stretched out on his back, impaled.

El Chicharrón had seen rightly. The capataz was dead. In one hand he held the rope by which he had caught his horse. The rope was wound tightly around his wrist, so that it would not come loose, no matter how hard the horse pulled.

His eyes were open and glazed. His face wore an expression of horrible fright, as if during his last moment he had seen a ghost approaching.

Don Ramón ordered the boys to free the horse first and then lift the body.

They had to pull the body and move it this way and that way to free it from the stake.

The caballeros examined the stake.

"A rare accident," Don Ramón said. "But things like that do happen. I remember, when I was a kid I saw something like this."

The stake was the thin trunk of a young tree of iron-hard wood. The peons, in their search for saplings to build the protecting roofs with, cut such stems off with a single blow of their machetes. This blow was never dealt at right angles to the side, but at a slant from top to bottom. So there remained a long slanted cut of some fifteen inches along the trunk above the ground. This cut was as sharp as the end of a spear. Anybody trying to find his way in the darkness of night, who stumbled and fell heavily on a stump of hard timber cut this way, would be helplessly impaled. If he had just roped a horse that shied away, pulling hard the very moment it felt the rope around its neck, it would drag the man at the other end of the rope deeper onto the stake.

Don Albán spat, crossed himself and said: "This spectacle is just as repulsive and gruesome as the one of that other rascal, what was his name, oh, yes, El Zorro. Well, señores, you'll pardon me but I can't hang around here doing nothing. It's late. Excuse me, I'll get my horse and be on my way."

Don Ramón hesitated for a moment. Then he said: "No use standing around here like old hags. We can't revive him. He's ice-cold already. Must have got speared early in the night. Horrible death. And how he stares! Judging from the way he stares at us, I would swear that by this time he's already cooking in hell. Anyway, I'm feeling kind of lousy around my belly. And right on top of my breakfast, too."

Don Gabriel lit a cigarette. "We'd better bury him, I think."

"Of course," said Don Gervasio, another of the traders. "Of course we'll have to bury him. Of course. What else is there to do? We can't very well take him along. In two hours, he'll be stinking. Well, I'm off, señores. Got to stick to my merchandise. I can't afford to lose it."

By now it was full day.

Don Ramón pulled himself together. "Now listen here, Don Gabriel, I'm going along with the troop. I can't leave the troop alone, you know that. If we hang around here looking at each other like idiots we'll get only as far as el paraje Cafetera today. And there we've got no water. Only a putrid pool, yellow, slimy, full of tadpoles. Not even thirsty mules touch that pestiferous pool. We have to get to Santa Clara, to the lake. Good, fresh spring water. I'm on my way, Don Gabriel. You finish up this business here. Santísima Madre del Dios Poderoso, ruega por mí." He crossed himself and stumbled off hastily back to the trail, where some boys were waiting with the horses.

"Empty his pockets," Don Gabriel ordered the peons who

stood around to help with the burial. "Has he any letters on him or other papers?"

"Nada de papeles, jefecito," replied El Chicharrón.

"Then the counting list must be in the saddlebag. You may divide up among you what he's got," Don Gabriel told El Chicharrón. "But first bury him and fight over the inheritance afterward."

"May I take the ring off, jefe?" asked El Chicharrón.

"You can put it on."

El Chicharrón spit on El Camarón's finger and, with great difficulty, managed to pull off the ring. He looked at it for a while and then put it on his own finger. It only fit his middle finger. The boys were already digging a hole for the corpse.

"Let me see that ring, Chicharrón," Don Gabriel said suddenly. El Chicharrón pulled the ring off again and handed it to Don Gabriel with an air of disappointment.

"Help the boys with the burial, so we won't lose so much time," he ordered. "Pull off his boots and see whether he had any money or papers in them."

"We've done that already, jefe," shouted one of the boys. "Nothing in them. The soles are full of holes, and the leather is split along one of the seams."

Don Gabriel looked critically at the ring, breathed on it and polished it on his shirt sleeve. He looked carefully at the inside of the large stone to see whether it had any backing or whether it was mounted free. Then he weighed the ring in his hand calculatingly. Again he rubbed it against his shirt sleeve and scratched at the stone with his pocket knife.

Finally he shoved the ring upon his finger and looked at his hand with satisfaction, stretching the finger and turning it in every direction. He clicked his tongue and mumbled: "Who would have thought it. I'd like to know where that scoundrel picked it up. Killed someone to get it, I wouldn't be surprised."

He pulled the ring from his finger and put it in his pocket.

After a while he fished it out again. Thoughtfully and with great care he knotted it into his bandanna.

"Aren't you lazy rascals ready yet?" he shouted furiously, and kicked the nearest of the men so hard in the behind that he took a dive head first into the excavation. "I'll get some movement into you if you've been thinking that you came here to sleep. Vamos, rápido! The devil knows when we'll catch up with the troop." He stamped around, lit a fresh cigarette, tapped the knot of his bandanna where the ring was, went a few paces to one side, came back, approached the excavation and said: "That's deep enough. The jabalíes will scent him anyway. Also the tigers. Roll him in. But first take his bandanna off."

"Here it is, jefe."

Don Gabriel spread the bandanna, shook it, approached the grave and laid it over the man's face. Through the bandanna he pressed on the eyes to close them. He straightened up, made the sign of the cross and said: "Virgencita Purísima, pray for us today and forever. Amen." He made one sign of the cross over the body and three over his own face, then kissed his right thumb.

He bent down, picked up a handful of earth, threw it on the body and said: "Cover him up. And you, Chicharrón, make a little cross."

"Here it is, jefecito," replied the Indian.

"Bueno, stick it in. Not there, you idiot. At the head end. And now, on your way and push your arses with your legs or I'll teach you how to run."

Out on the trail he ordered El Chicharrón to lead El Camarón's horse by the rope. He himself mounted his own horse, waited until all the men had slung the straps of their packs over their foreheads, let them march past him and then rode off, keeping his horse so close to the last man that the small group had to fall into a trot to avoid being pushed by the horse.

"Well, at last I'm going to show you how to march," he said. "Until today you had no idea what marching really means."

In two hours they caught up with the main troop.

32

This day the caravan had to march nearly ten leguas. It was indeed a hard day.

Around noon, they arrived at the Desempeño River, where the troop stopped for a short rest. The muchachos whom Don Gabriel had taught marching dropped as if shot. Don Ramón saw it, walked up to them and said: "If you start running like wild men, you'll never reach the monterías." From his morral in which he, like every Mexican horseman, kept the day's ration, he took a tin of sardines, threw it to the panting men and said: "Divide it among you, and don't drink so much water. That won't do you any good."

Later he said to Don Gabriel: "Amigo, there's something you'll have to learn in this business. It isn't enough to catch men. You have to deliver them to the monterías in good health and with plenty of strength. Otherwise you won't get paid for them. No cash, you know."

"It won't do them any harm if you shake them up once in a while," replied Don Gabriel. "They're like goats."

"As you like," replied Don Ramón calmly. "I only wanted you to know. Throughout my life I've handled contract workers. In my younger years I recruited men for the silver, zinc and copper mines. All laborers, without any exception, have a definite limit to their strength, their efficiency and their good will. If you drive them beyond that, one of two things will happen: either they become dangerous or they become useless. Neither will do us any good."

Don Gabriel said: "Perhaps you are right, Don Ramón, but, you see, I wanted to get away from that terrible sight there—get away from it as far as possible and as fast as I could make it."

While he was saying that Don Albán came strolling along. "Señores," he said, "I'm feeling terribly uneasy. It seems to me as if we are marching through the jungle eternally, as if we are running in a circle. Not once today did we have the open sky over us. Green and dark, and dark and green. And this broiling heat and this oppressive humidity. And the eternal whispering and chirping around us and that horrible yelling of the gritones which hammers at us day and night. If I don't soon see a house, a table, a plate and, above all, a few different faces in front of my eyes, por la Santísima, I'll go crazy. Why in the name of God did I have to stick my nose into trading in the monterías?"

Don Ramón laughed and slapped him hard on his back. "Don't talk so much rot, Don Albán. Everything will pass. And once you've sold everything you're dragging along, with a one hundred, in some cases with a two hundred per cent profit, you'll think differently of the jungle. Don't brood. Whistle yourself a song. We also have no woman along, no more than you. That's all that's the matter with you. I've become accustomed to it. Well, señores, on our horses."

He pulled out his whistle and gave the signal to march.

Around five o'clock in the afternoon the troop sensed the first signs of the great lake in the surrounding air. A soft wind carried the smell of rushes, of rotting lake grass, of muddy and swampy banks up to the steep slope from which the caravan was winding its way down toward the lake. At times, one saw the lake and the wide-open space above it blinking through a clearing in the jungle.

The trail was broken and, at times, hardly more than two and a half feet wide. But even if one slipped, neither man nor beast could fall down the abyss, because the high, massive rocky mountain was densely covered with trees, shrubs and bushes.

The caravan marched in a long file, man after man, animal after animal. None could stop. It would have held up the whole troop. Some of the animals slipped now and then. Without causing a halt they were immediately supported by the ever watchful arrieros who now pushed, now pulled them back onto the path.

The nearer the caravan came to the lake, the faster the animals marched. The last quarter of an hour they even trotted, in spite of their packs, not minding their saddle-galled backs, oblivious to their fatigue.

Notwithstanding the terrific noise made by the lake birds, there was about the lake itself and all around it a loneliness that was both mysterious and oppressive. There was no apparent reason for it, yet it weighed inexplicably upon man's mind.

Large grazing grounds to which oxen, working in the monterías, were sent every three months for a rest, encircled the lake. The mahogany workers labored in the monterías day in, day out, month after month, year after year until finally they were buried there except for the small number who survived their contracts. Yet never were they given a day's vacation. The oxen lost weight and vitality, even died unless they were periodically rested in the pastures several days' march away from the monterías of which they had become weary.

The camp site was wide open. One could see the whole sky above. After so many days in the monotony of the dark green jungle thicket it seemed like the awakening from a nightmare. But three hours later the torment began—a torment so intense that one was ready to renounce all the beauties and enchantment of the lake and its picturesque surroundings. Because of the many oxen grazing here, the entire camp site was infested by millions and millions of garrapatas. Within one hour everybody had his clothes and his body so full of ticks that he gave up all resistance and let himself be bitten wherever it pleased the insects. Bathing in the lake unfortunately did not kill them but refreshed them just as it did men. Anyway it was next to impossible to take a swim. The banks, from about two hundred yards inward, were swampy and covered with dense rushes. Therefore, one was even deprived of a refreshing bath.

The drinking water was not gotten from the lake but instead from two springs which gushed forth at the foot of high rocks situated close to the lake.

In the evening, when they were squatting at the fire, Celso said to Andrés: "I foretold that El Camarón would meet with a little accident right at this rocky wall where we get such cool and clear water. But fate wouldn't have it this way. You see, one can't count on fate entirely and one should also never even try to improve on fate. Leave it alone. It acts in its own way."

"Did you hear," asked Andrés, "what the boys who buried him said about the accident—that it couldn't have been an accident, not with so smart a guy as that bastard was?"

"If I were to listen to the rattle of those halfwits I would never have a thought of my own," Celso replied. "After all, what do I care about such a dirty cabrón? But I tell you, one thing is sure like the sun, he and that other whoremonger El Zorro won't hook another Indio and drag him away from his woman. All I can do is spit heartily when I think of those two crabs."

Next day the march led through a dense section of the jungle which was of an entirely different nature from the one the caravan had crossed during the previous days. Not for fifty paces did the trail lead over firm, sandy or stony ground. All was mud, swamp, march with not the slightest variation.

Celso, marching besides Andrés, said: "Well, manito, now you can smell caoba all around you, even though you don't yet see a single tree. But actually you're already inside the caoba empire. Tonight you'll see the first remains of a great abandoned montería and a few other things to reflect upon provided you haven't lost the capacity to think and reflect."

The flora was changing completely. The change was so noticeable that not only the peons who walked through there for the first time observed it, but even the traders, who usually paid not much attention to plants and trees along the trail, looked up. To them, as a rule, a tree was a tree and a bush was a bush. Whether it was an ebony tree or a mango tree or a fraile was absolutely immaterial to them as long as none of the trees they saw bought any of their merchandise. There was no reason why they should be interested in the sight of a tree or in its value.

The saddle horses and the pack mules slipped and sank into the deep, muddy soil at every step. Carefully feeling their way, they were permanently on the lookout for the driest spots where they could gain a firm foothold.

It was always the rainy season in these regions. If you ask an old, experienced montería contractor to tell you when the rainy season begins and when the dry season sets in, with a poker face he will answer: "Yes, señor, here our rainy season begins approximately on the fifteenth of June." Then comes the unavoidable question: "And when does the rainy season end in this region?" And the reply, given with the same indifference: "Around midnight on the fourteenth of June."

This was true. Even if it did not rain during the early morning, there was such a heavy dew in the jungle that, whether one marched or rode on horseback, until noon one was constantly soaked to the skin by the water dropping from trees and bushes. About one o'clock or so it started to dry, and around two o'clock the tropical rain would begin to pour down, without interruption, for four to six hours. No wonder then that the trail here was like a plowed potato field after six weeks' constant rain.

Wherever one looked there were fan palms and bush palms. The feathery leaves sprouted from the palms right near the roots, so it seemed that these palms had no regular trunk. And because the feathery leaves did not grow high up along the trunk, but came right out of the soil, the jungle was so thick that one could rightly say, "You can't see the jungle because of the palms."

In fact, it was a wild, nightmarish matting of plants of pre-historic times. Many of the palm feathers were one hundred feet high. And there were thousands of ferns of equal height. One could not see the ground beside the trail, so heavily was it grown over with matting. Deep in one's mind one perceived the merciless battle of the plants each fighting the other. All around, one beheld a ruthless rivalry, a relentless struggle for a piece of space as small as a child's hand. Men's strife for ex-istence could hardly be waged more inflexibly than the battle among the plants in this wide area.

This was the very earth which conceived caoba, gave birth to caoba and developed caoba to its full splendor, vitality and strength. For this aristocratic timber can attain its beauty, its full consistency and its hardness only where it has to fight cruelly and pitilessly for its existence and survival. Whatever is conceived here, and once conceived grows and survives, has to be of a truly heroic nature. Softness and timidity are stamped into the mud to rot. The one that loses the battle serves as fer-tilizer for the one of greater beauty, strength and nobility.

"Look around, manito," Celso said to Andrés, who was marching, as though in a dream, through this enchanted world which had struck his sensibility as something entirely new and absolutely unexpected. "Look around I say again. Here it begins, the vast, savage land of caoba. Perhaps for the first time now you'll understand why man cannot harvest caoba like any odd crop in the fields of a finca. I've planted coffee in Soconusco, in some kind of selva, some sort of jungle. You see, coffee is planted like any other valuable crop, with special care, in this particular case under huge trees. Otherwise there isn't much difference between maize, coffee, beans, oats, cacahuates, chiles or what have you. But now here, caoba, that's something else again. And believe you me, now that I'm back here once more, smelling caoba, I honestly think that I really couldn't live anywhere else. I almost believe that I was truly homesick for caoba.

"After all, tell me, mano, what and where is the meaning of my life? The woman? The fifteen children? The wool, the chicken, the pigs, the maize, the fuel, the beans to be hauled to market? You can get goddamn sick and tired of that, too, so that you want to run away from it. I'm lost, I tell you, I'm lost. I belong here. To hell with the fifteen brats. And be careful, manito, that the same doesn't happen to you someday."

33

It went on for hours. It was as if an entirely new
world had begun and the old, known world had
sunk away. A new world had opened and this new world was
nothing but a confused, intertwined, matted mass of something
that grew. Grew and grew and grew. One lost the capacity of
distinguishing the individual plants. Anything and everything
around was green, thicket, abundance, confusion. Little golden
dwarfs of sunlight were continually dancing from one feathery palm leaf to another. It was as though over this solid dense
world of plants floated a call urging creation to beget a new
planet, a fantastic one in which not man or beast would be the
master but plants. One felt lonely and abandoned, separated
from all the remaining world, in spite of the long file of peons
and the grunting and snorting pack animals marching along
mechanically. The marchers, men and animals, seemed to move
without volition, almost dreamlike, into this world of plants to
be swallowed up by it.

Suddenly Andrés shouted: "Dios mío, what is—but that is—"
With a sudden lurch he halted, dropping his pack.

"But what is that?" he asked, panting.

Unexpectedly the jungle had opened before his eyes, and so

223

widely that in all directions new worlds extended toward the horizon. At the feet of the two young men, far below, there ran the river, the imposing, powerful, mysterious Ushumah-cintla River, the giant without whose assistance no mahogany could be taken out of these wild regions and brought to the civilized world. It was the visible god responsible for the Indios who were devoured by caoba. Without this majestic river of the jungle, caoba would have been as valueless as a rotting pine stick in the forests of North Dakota. And since caoba would be valueless nobody would sell Indios for their debts to work in the monterías.

Incomparable in its scope and its majesty was the view from this site, high over the banks, where the eye could follow the titanic river in its winding loops.

It was still early. Hardly two o'clock in the afternoon. And yet the order was given to camp. From here the first distribution of the laborers was made for the various monterías which needed new hands.

For several days the main troop would continue marching deeper into the jungle, yet remaining on this side of the river. Smaller troops were ferried across the river in canoes and taken to the monterías which were along the opposite bank.

The sons of Mexico who were canoed over to the opposite bank entered a foreign country without knowing it. They were swept under the sovereignty of another government without being consulted. The mahogany companies recognized neither nationalities nor citizens' rights, nor were they reluctant about kidnaping citizens of any country or trespassing on national borders. They only acknowledged the powerful Empire of the Caoba, which had no nationality. Where caoba ruled was the land where they reigned and where only those laws were respected which they themselves made and where they exercised the power to enforce their laws as they saw fit. They did not bother about concessions and their clauses. They did not worry about national frontiers, presidents of republics or dictators. All that was far away, infinitely far away. All that had vanished from the earth. They were separated from all that by two weeks of seemingly endless marches through the jungle. Whoever arrived here became small and insignificant. He simply had, without being asked, invaded the sacred land where caoba was the dictator, the supreme law.

None of Celso's group thought of lighting a fire. There was plenty of time for that. The day would last for many hours. They just squatted there, comfortable and satisfied that they could rest.

They had chosen a place apart from the main troop, farther down on an elevation from where one could have a clear view of the river and of its high banks.

"How beautiful, how impressive that great river is," said Celso suddenly. "This in itself is worth the march to the monterías even if only to rot there. See those pretty sandy beaches? Later, shortly before sunset, let's go down for a swim. It will do us good."

"What are those huts over there on the opposite bank?" asked Andrés.

"That's a montería," Celso said. "What you see there is the administration building and the jacalitos for the employees and some artisans. The montería proper is deep in the jungle. You can't see it from here."

He looked around and saw the main troop getting busy pitching camp. "Well," he said musingly while rolling himself a long and very thick cigar, "the soldiers have finally arrived. Here is where the battlefields begin. Right here at this site there also used to be a montería in times gone by. Why!" he interrupted his speech, "I just remembered, do you want to see something awfully interesting? Hey you, greenies," he shouted to a bigger group nearby, "you, too, come along with me and get an eyeful."

He led them a short way downstream, turned to the left, passing with some difficulty through a thicket of brush, and there, before their eyes, was spread out a wide field of little mounds, many of them marked by crudely made crosses. Wiry grass and thorny shrubs were growing all over the place. However, one hundred and fifty, if not more, of those little mounds could still be fairly well distinguished. The great majority of crosses had rotted away and the rest crumbled. Most of the mounds were eroded or had leveled out. From their look one could see that they had been scratched open by hungry wild hogs or other animals of the jungle.

"What's this here?" Santiago asked, perplexed and frightened at the same time. "It looks like a—like a—but then here in this lonely place? How come?"

"Yes, here in this lonely place where nearby a montería used to be," said Celso impassively. "Yes, here is where the fallen caoba men of that now almost forgotten montería found their last paraje. You'll march deeper into caoba land, into the caoba empire, and you will have other surprises, real surprises which will make you gasp for breath. One thing I can tell you. Unless you become like caoba, hard as steel, and get dark red blood into your veins, you also will soon find your last paraje near one or another montería. Here you have to fight tooth and claw against capataces, against whippings and hangings, and above all against the jungle that wants to devour you." He paused. "Aw, damn it! Forget it! Stop thinking about it. Makes no sense standing here gazing at those bones you see lying about. The men to whom they belonged won't cough again."

For a few seconds his eyes rested on a particular little mound which by its appearance seemed less old than most of the others. He lifted his arm as though he intended to point at this singular heap of sand and perhaps say something about it. But he merely bit hard on his lip, turned abruptly away and shouted: "Say, cuates, let's cook our beans and have them well mixed with chile verde y muchas yerbas. And you"—now addressing a small group of youngsters standing around with their mouths wide open—"don't you greenhorns dream of home or any such nonsense. No good for you. I'm telling you. It's poison and you should know it. Forget it. Better fetch some fuel and build a lusty fire."

Rose-colored birds were circling inquisitively over the camp. Perceiving no danger, they spiraled in wide arcs toward the sandy banks of the majestic river, finally glided down, walked leisurely on their long, thin legs as if on stilts into the slowly flowing water and began, rather solemnly, to fish.

FOR THIRTY-FIVE YEARS, *from 1876 to 1911, power in Mexico was in the hands of one man, Porfirio Díaz. Mexico's constitution had been altered to give sanction to his re-elections, which were assured by his appointment of state governors and other officials. Opposition was controlled by a ruthless federal police, called the* rurales. *It was a reign of peace and prosperity for the few and dire poverty for the many—half the entire rural population of Mexico was bound to debt slavery. Big landowners and foreign capital were favored as more and more Indians lost their communal lands.*

In the final decade of Díaz' rule, however, opposition strengthened, and before his last engineered re-election he promised a return to democratic forms—which after the election he gave no sign of honoring. In 1910 revolution broke out; independent rebel armies under the leadership of Pancho Villa, Emiliano Zapata, Francisco Madero and others upset the power of the landlords and eventually overthrew the Díaz regime.

In what have become known as the "Jungle Novels," B. Traven *wrote, during the 1930's, an epic of the birth of the Mexican revolution. The six novels*—Government, The Carreta, March to the Montería, The Troza, The Rebellion of the Hanged, *and* The General from the Jungle—*describe the conditions of peonage and debt slavery under which the Indians suffered in Díaz' time. The novels follow the spirit of rebellion that slowly spread through the labor camps and haciendas, culminating in the bloody revolt that ended Porfirio Díaz' rule.*

In the 1920's, when B. Traven arrived in the country, peonage, although officially abolished by the new constitution of 1917, was still a general practice in many parts of Mexico. The author observed the system at first hand in Chiapas, the south-ernmost province, a mountainous and heavily forested region, where the jungle novels, as well as many other of his stories, are set.

ALLISON & BUSBY FICTION

Simon Beckett
Fine Lines
Animals

Philip Callow
The Magnolia
The Painter's Confessions

Catherine Heath
Lady on the Burning Deck
Behaving Badly

Chester Himes
Cast the First Stone
Collected Stories
The End of a Primitive
Pink Toes
Run Man Run

Tom Holland
Attis

R. C. Hutchinson
A Child Possessed
Johanna at Daybreak
Recollection of a Journey

Dan Jacobson
The Evidence of Love

Francis King
Act of Darkness
The One and Only
The Widow

Colin MacInnes
Absolute Beginners
City of Spades
Mr Love and Justice
The Colin MacInnes Omnibus

Indira Mahindra
The End Play

Susanna Mitchell
The Colour of His Hair

Bill Naughton
Alfie

Matthew Parkhill
And I Loved Them Madly

Alison Prince
The Witching Tree

Ishmael Reed
Japanese by Spring
Reckless Eyeballing
The Terrible Threes
The Terrible Twos
The Free-Lance Pallbearers
Yellow Back Radio Broke-Down

Françoise Sagan
Engagements of the Heart
Evasion
Incidental Music
The Leash
The Unmade Bed

Budd Schulberg
The Disenchanted
The Harder They Fall
Love, Action, Laughter and
    Other Sad Stories
On the Waterfront
What Makes Sammy Run?

Debbie Taylor
The Children Who Sleep
    by the River

B. Traven
Government
The Carreta
Trozas

Etienne Van Heerden
Ancestral Voices
Mad Dog and Other Stories

Tom Wakefield
War Paint